BROKEN SKIES

DRAGON'S GIFT: THE STORM BOOK 4

VERONICA DOUGLAS

LINSEY HALL

For our parents, here and gone.

© 2021 Magic Side Press

Magic Side Press

MAGIC SIDE, CHICAGO

Gilbart Rock
Breakers
Bentham Prison
Shoreline
The Circuit
Flyby
Hall of Inquiry
Exposition Park
Midway Den
Hideout
Hyde Park
Dockside Dens
Jackson Park
Old Mud City
The Flats
South Shore
The Indies
South Chicago

WELCOME TO MAGIC SIDE, CHICAGO!
Having trouble getting around?
Ride Magic Side Surface Lines
Always efficient, always free!
Buy One Dog Get One Free
Sammy's Italian Gelato
& Chicago Dogs
(limit one per customer)

1

———

Neve

The engines of the boat whirred as we approached Bentham Island.

It had been three days since we'd broken the curse on the prison and banished Matthias's genies. The prison walls had been breached in the attack, and five prisoners had managed to escape. To say the situation was bad was an understatement. Bentham was a high-security jail that held the most dangerous Magica.

We bounced over a wave, and I tightened my grip on the cuffed devil hunched between Rhiannon and me. I'd be glad to hand him over to the Order.

The captain gripped the wheel, knuckles white, and eyes locked on the dock ahead. "I heard there's still one on the loose. A sorcerer or something of the sort. A real bad guy by the sounds of him."

Not our problem, fortunately.

The deckhand snorted and gestured at the devil. "They're all bad. The worst of Magica. I heard this one's nicknamed the Ripper."

A low chortle escaped the devil, and Rhia jabbed him with her elbow.

Fortunately, another Order detail had nabbed two other escapees this morning. The sooner we dropped this bastard off, the sooner I could sleep, shower, and get real sustenance. Possibly in a different order.

The devil watched me through a pair of cat-like eyes. He shifted, and the magicuffs on his wrists scraped against the wooden bench. We'd hunted him all night and had gotten lucky. If it weren't for the two bodies he'd left in the Dens, it might have gone differently.

The engines quieted, and the boat glided toward a dock that had seen better days. The concrete was pock-marked by the tsunami that had hit the island, and chunks of concrete and mortar littered the shore and shallows.

I squinted up at the translucent magic dome that protected the prison. It flickered in the early afternoon sun, and all traces of the dark curse that had plagued it just days ago had vanished.

The deckhand shuffled toward the bow, skirting beside Rhia and leaning as far from the devil as was possible without falling off the boat. He braced himself against the gunwale and peered into the glassy water as the boat inched forward. "Ten feet of water. No obstructions."

The captain maneuvered the boat alongside the dock, and the deckhand leapt ashore, deftly tying the mooring lines to two metal cleats.

Rhia turned to the devil and smirked. "Ready to go back to the pokie, Luci?"

"How about I rip your throat out first, beautiful?" the devil growled.

"Nope. Wrong answer." I stood and gripped the devil by his arm, wrenching him to his feet. He growled and hexed me under his breath. Under normal circumstances I might've been worried, but I was running on Twizzlers and gas station coffee alone, and after the week I'd just had, I didn't have any fucks left to give.

We dragged the devil onto the dock, and I glanced over my shoulder. "We'll be back in five."

The captain waved at me absently and resumed tending to the ropes.

"Whatcha say we grab a few dogs from Sammy's after this? I'm starving," Rhia said, the exhaustion clear in her voice. She was preaching to the choir. While there was still one more prisoner on the loose, he was the archmages's problem, not ours.

"Oh-my-gods-yes." My stomach grumbled at the image I'd conjured of Sammy's Chicago dogs, then I winced at the thought of the tab I probably now owed.

Since returning with me from the Realm of Fire, my

familiar, Spark, had developed a taste for hot dogs. Well, *for their essence.* He was a fire sprite who liked to take the form of a dragon, and he had an unusually big appetite and a knack for thieving—

The devil suddenly shrieked, jerked out of my grip, and swung for Rhia's jaw. With cat-like reflexes, she deflected the blow and kneed him in the balls. The devil spat, leapt over our heads, and raced toward the concrete-littered shore.

Red hot rage bubbled in my chest, and I savored the feeling as it spread through me, savagely wonderful. Focusing on the devil, I released my breath in a silent puff. A gust of wind rocketed forward, ramming the bastard into the ground. Delight streaked through me, and I strode forward, raising a hand.

The devil shuffled across the dirt like a wounded animal, fear coloring his face.

"You want to run off and leave a few more bodies, is that it? I can leave one right here." My vision homed in on him like a predator on its prey, and I clenched my fist, enjoying the sting of my nails digging into my palm. The devil clutched his throat and flopped onto his back. His chest heaved as he gasped for air.

"Neve." Rhiannon appeared at my side and gently gripped my shoulder. "Stop."

Her words echoed through my mind, drawing me back to my senses. I opened my fist, releasing my magic. The devil sucked in air, his skin ashen.

Guilt and shame churned in my stomach. This wasn't who I was. I shook my head, trying to rid myself of the haze. "Sorry. I don't know what got into me."

Rhiannon squeezed my shoulder and dragged the cowering prisoner to his feet. "Come on, you bastard."

She glanced back at me and nodded toward the three guards who were standing at the gate, gawking.

Crap. They'd seen that. Not ideal.

The devil put up little resistance as Rhia towed him to the gate and handed him to the guards. She flashed them a wide smile and shook her head, gesturing back at me with her thumb. "Mages, huh? Always showing off."

The guards looked between Rhia and me with blank faces before escorting the devil through the prison's doors. Nobody but a handful of my friends and my boss knew what I was, and I had to keep it that way—an order from Gretchen, my boss.

"Have a good one!" Rhia shouted after them, then turned to me. "That was awesome. But next time, I might suggest using a little more restraint."

"Fates, the anger just came out of nowhere." Archmage DeLoren had warned me about losing control of my emotions, but I had no idea it would be this bad. It was like my feelings and my magic were interwoven.

Rhia shimmied and shook her arms dramatically. "Ugh. Glad that's done with. That one gave me the creeps."

"Really? More so than the heart-eater?" She was a serial killer witch. We'd caught her yesterday trying to make her way over the bridge to Chicago. She'd made a habit of carving out the hearts of her exes and eating them. Raw.

Rhia shrugged. "Bastards probably had it coming."

Possibly. The witch's victims *had* had a history of battery and stalking.

We picked our way through the wreckage toward the waiting boat.

The spire of Malek Tower rose above the Circuit's skyscrapers, a beacon directing my gaze. Or a spear piercing the heavens. Regret, grief, and anger filled the emptiness in my chest.

Damian Malek. The source of so much of my pain and anger, and yet, I couldn't stop thinking about him.

I hadn't seen Damian since the battle for Bentham. We'd only spoken once, and he'd made his desire for distance very clear. It was for the best—or at least that's what I'd tried to tell myself. One thing was certain—our relationship would not end happily ever after because whatever he felt for me, his FireSoul cravings were, apparently, stronger.

I couldn't help but recall the fire in his eyes when he'd ripped the efreet's magic from its corpse. That could be me.

But somehow, I couldn't reconcile that image with the man who'd saved my life, time and time again.

Who'd idiotically thrown himself in harm's way to protect me from the hydra.

Rhia sighed audibly. "You're thinking about *him*, aren't you?"

Nausea churned my stomach. "Is it really that obvious?"

"Lately, yes. You're like a freaking picture book when it comes to your emotions."

"Oh gods." I frowned and rubbed my temples. I really did have to learn to rein in my emotions *and* my magic.

"Let's focus on the positives, though. One, you saved Magic Side and banished two lunatic genies. Two, you have a dragon familiar who is ridiculously cute and deadly." She paused and scrunched her brows together and then smiled. "Oh yeah, and three. You're a freaking full-blown djinn now. In my book, that makes you one badass bitch."

I couldn't help but laugh. Rhia wasn't the glass-half-full kinda girl, but the glass-is-overflowing-and-you-need-to-take-a-big-sip-from-the-edge-so-you-don't-spill-it kind. She was my best friend, and we'd been through a lot together.

While she might be right about a few things, I still couldn't shake my anxiety. Becoming a full djinn had always been my biggest fear, and now that it had happened, I simultaneously loved and feared it. Having this much power was...well, there were no words to describe it.

But, as my outburst moments ago had indicated, my new powers were volatile and deeply linked with my emotions. If I didn't learn how to temper both, who knew what kind of destruction I might unleash.

Memories of my old neighborhood forced their way into my thoughts. The ruined apartment, overturned cars, and wind-toppled trees.

Much of the destruction had been the efreet's fault, but much was also mine—collateral damage of my rage and single-minded desire to destroy him.

But I'd done what I needed to save my city.

Dread crept along my spine, but I forced a smile for Rhiannon. She'd carried me through a lot. "Yeah, well, I'm a badass bitch with a big fat target on my back."

And that was the truth. When I'd become a full djinn, I gained the power to grant wishes. But it meant that a powerful spellcaster could bind me to an enchanted object, like a lamp or a bottle, and force me to grant wishes against my will.

I'd rather die than let that happen.

Rhiannon shrugged. "True. Matthias is probably coming for you, but we're going to be ready for the demon bastard. I'll stop time. You punch him really hard in the face."

I snorted, unintentionally. There were benefits to having a friend who could manipulate time. And it would feel really good to cold-cock Matthias. The treacherous bastard was *definitely* coming for me. I was pretty sure he'd expected me to eventually turn into a full djinn, biding his time until he could trap me.

Rhiannon shot me a furtive glance. "Have you spoken with Damian? Maybe he can help."

I tensed at the sound of his name. Fallen angel and FireSoul. A deep ache settled in my chest, right beside the mounting irritation.

"We've only spoken once since we banished the marid. It was the shortest conversation of my life. Damian said he couldn't control his FireSoul craving, and it was too dangerous to be around me. That was that. He hung up without listening to anything I had to say." The words were like pouring acid into a wound.

We'd been through hell together and, despite the lies and betrayal, he'd always had my back. The unfortunate truth was, we couldn't be together because he craved my magic and might kill me for it—now more so than ever since, in order to save him, I'd had to become a full djinn.

The irony of that stung.

Rhia snorted. "Seriously? That guy needs a twelve-step program. FireSouls Anonymous. Hell, maybe the vampires have a program he could enroll in."

I choked out a half-hearted laugh and squeezed Rhia's hand as we crossed the dock toward the waiting boat. "If only. But it's better if he stays away. It's what I want."

Lie.

It may have been what my mind wanted, but my body definitely had other plans.

In the end, it was his eyes that hooked me, deep green, like staring up through a forest of pines. His eyes, his signature, his whiskey voice. Actually, pretty much every part of him, if I were being honest.

That night on the shore of Apollonia had felt so right, I couldn't ignore it. He was the first thing on my mind when I woke each morning, and it took a long time to clear my head afterward. Usually in the shower.

Traitorous thoughts.

The fallen angel was trouble, and he knew it.

Rhiannon cocked her brow at me. "Right. Well, in the meantime, let's do some old-fashioned sleuthing. Where can we get answers about Matthias?"

We climbed into the boat and took a seat near the bow. I raised my voice over the rumble of the engines. "I've been thinking about that—he's damned good at covering his tracks. His house and possessions are currently burnt to a crisp, and forensics have gone over the rubble with a fine-toothed comb, but maybe you can use your power to look into the past?"

Rhia cracked a wicked grin at me. "Abso-freakin-lutely."

Gods, I loved her. The fates may have cursed my

chances with Damian, but at least I had Rhia. We'd been friends for a decade. More than friends—she was all the family I had.

I'd accidently planes-walked away from my parents when I was a child. I'd never found my way back to them, and they'd never come for me.

For a long time, I'd just assumed they were dead.

That assumption had changed two and half weeks ago in the Realm of Air. The djinn that abducted Rhiannon said something that made me think they were still alive. He'd been taunting me, but there'd been a hint of truth in his words. I could feel it in my bones.

I'd been doing my best not to think about it—trying not to get my hopes up. But maybe if we defeated Matthias, I could force the djinn to tell me where they were, or at least, what he knew.

As the captain navigated the boat out of the anchorage, a second engine rumbled to life, breaking me out of my reverie.

I looked back. A few hundred feet offshore, a gunboat wheeled around the side of the island and began following us. It was not unlike the one from the Dockside Dens that Lily DuVoir had arrived on a few days ago. I counted five guys in it, all dressed in black tactical gear.

My heart had leapt for just a second, but it wasn't Matthias. The bastard would have shown up from the skies with demons. Not in a boat with thugs.

Irritation prickled my skin, and I glared at the captain. "When did they show up? And how come you didn't tell us there was someone anchored out of sight?"

The captain winced. "I heard them pull up about ten minutes ago. They were obscured by the prison walls. I initially assumed they were just tourists snapping some pictures of Bentham, but it doesn't look like it. Should I call it in?"

I blinked twice. Tourists my ass. Those guys were definitely following us, and I was pretty sure I knew who they worked for.

"That bastard," I murmured.

2

———

Neve

Our boat glided up to the docks in North Channel Harbor.

I glared at the guys in the boat, which pulled up alongside the adjacent wharf. They were dressed in tactical pants and black shirts, and judging by the hints of pine and sweat, I'd bet they were shifters. Werewolves probably.

"Some tourists, huh?" Rhia raised her brows at the captain.

"Not my problem." The captain shrugged as the deckhand grabbed hold of a cleat and inched the boat forward.

"Typical." Rhia let out an exasperated sigh and climbed onto the concrete wharf. I followed, still glaring as the stalkers secured their mooring lines and leapt out of the boat.

"You two be careful, now," the deckhand said as he pushed off the dock and the captain throttled the engine.

"Let me guess. Damian's thugs?" Rhiannon said, glancing back at the stalkers as we marched across the docks.

"No doubt," I said bitterly, pulling out my phone and dialing *him*.

I was pretty sure he'd hired a security team to follow me around the city. I'd caught a whiff of them last night but thought we'd lost them.

Yet here they were.

Damian's phone rang twice and then went straight to voicemail. Did he just screen my call?

The complete and utter ass.

I typed out a text and hit send: *Call off your goons.*

The message went through, and my adrenaline spiked when I noticed the three dots moving beneath his name. The bastard was writing back.

Not a chance. Matthias and his genies are hunting you. You need protection.

Reading the text, I clenched my phone and shoved it in my pocket.

A little heads up would have been nice.

As much as I hated having Damian's men following

me and reporting my every move back to him, I had a target on my back and appreciated the protection.

Rhia grinned while taking in the shifters' measures. "Well, at least they're not terrible looking."

I scowled because she was right. They were all built like brick houses and hunky as all hell. But I had eyes for only one man, and I was pretty sure that if he were here right now, I would tear him a new one. And then maybe jump his bones. Right before he killed me.

Clearly, my body wasn't into thinking through consequences.

Rhia unlocked the doors of our official silver cruiser. There were perks to being an Order detective, but I couldn't fully appreciate them with the hot flaming mess I was currently wrapped up in.

We climbed in, and Rhia started the car. "Matthias's house is in the Gaslight District, right?"

"That's right. The address is 6300 Stone Haven." I'd been there a few times when it was still standing. That was before I'd discovered that Matthias was the treacherous bastard behind the stolen genies and the attacks on Magic Side.

"Okay, we'll check it out, but we're going to Sammy's right after this. Deal?" Rhia gave me a pointed look.

"Deal." I peered into the side mirror as we pulled out of the marina parking lot. The shifters were following us in a black SUV. Irritation prickled the back of my neck, even if having backup wasn't the worst idea. I just wished that backup had been somebody else.

Ugh. I needed to stop thinking about Damian. He. Could. Kill. Me. It would be insane to think otherwise.

Wouldn't it?

The morning traffic had eased up, and we made it to Matthias's house—or at least what was left of it—in under ten minutes.

We needed to figure out what Matthias was up to. He was after me, for certain. But I was only one piece of the puzzle. He'd used his genies to create a new elemental plane—a Realm of Chaos—and was assembling an army of demons. Why, I wasn't exactly sure, but there's a chance he was planning to invade the city.

It wasn't just my freedom at stake. It was all of Magic Side.

Rhia parked alongside the curb. Ignoring the shifters who pulled up behind us, I stepped up to the twisted remains of the wrought-iron fence that once surrounded the yard. Two pieces of torn, yellow police tape blew in the gentle breeze.

"Can't believe the Order hasn't cleaned this mess up yet." Rhia stopped beside me.

"Guess they've had their hands full. Lucky for us."

We picked our way through the wreckage, searching for anything that might be useful. But all that remained were brick and mortar and a few pieces of splintered furniture. Matthias had likely taken everything of importance before destroying the house—though I bet the bastard hadn't anticipated us looking into the past.

I grinned at Rhiannon. "Ready to do your thing?"

Rhia was a time traveler. While she still hadn't mastered the whole traveling into the past part, she could look into it, and even slow the present down. It was a pretty badass ability, though it didn't come without its risks.

Rhia crouched and closed her eyes, resting her palm on a charred brick. The wind picked up, and the police tape danced in the air, making a cracking sound. Two of the hot shifters leaned against the black SUV and watched us closely.

"Holy shit," Rhia whispered. As the curse left her lips, the air vibrated with energy and a thunderous crack rang out.

"Was that your magic?" I said, clutching my ringing ears. If so, I'd never seen that happen before.

"No." Rhiannon stood, worry tugging at the corners of her mouth. "Uh, Neve."

My heartbeat quickened, and I followed her gaze to the far corner of the building. The scent of smoke and hot iron burned my nose. My body tensed.

"Good morning, Nevaeh." Matthias stood between two demons with sickly green skin and hollow eyes. Their hellish appearance was a bizarre contrast to his precise style, consisting of a striped shirt tucked neatly into dark, pressed trousers. "And this must be the blonde friend that the djinn has told me so much about. So nice to finally make your acquaintance."

"Asshole." The wind picked up around me, and the tattoos that wound over my chest and arms itched as my magic flared to life.

Growls erupted from behind, and a massive black wolf stepped into my periphery. *Holy heck.* The wolf bared its teeth, and its fur bristled. Holy shit. I'd gotten used to Gretchen shifting, but this guy was on another level.

"You brought wolves," Matthias sneered, a look of disgust painted on his fucking face. "Well, I brought something of yours."

My heart plummeted, and fear took root as Matthias pulled his hands from behind his back. In the right, he held an enchanted bottle. In the left, my old khanjar. The two components needed to bind a genie—a powerful receptacle, and an object treasured by the djinn.

My gut clenched. This was it.

I whipped my hands up and blasted the bottle and khanjar out of his hands with precise jets of air.

He leapt into the air on black wings and cried "Ascaranda bettayo."

Say what now?

The demons surged forward as Matthias flicked his wrist and my old khanjar leapt back into his hand—he was an iron mage with mastery over metal.

The black wolf to my right launched into the air, tearing out the throat of the closest adversary. Dark blood dribbled out of the wolf's jaws. It shook the demon in his mouth and slung the body into the piles of burnt brick.

Damn, these wolves were badass.

Mind-bending screeches filled the air as more demons leapt from behind the ruins and charged over the rubble in an unnatural, four-legged run. These fuckers were scary as all hell.

Wolves leapt up on either side of us, ripping into the demons. A hellish corpse slammed to the ground at my feet, and I leapt back as it melted into black smoke. The problem with demons was that they didn't die when you killed them. Their bodies regenerated in the underworld, and unless they'd been banished with a spell, they'd likely return.

"Seriously, Matthias?" Rhiannon screamed, kicking the feet of a demon. "You brought demons to do your dirty work?"

Another attacked from behind. Rhia loosed her magic bolas named Hercules. The two balls whipped through the air and wrapped around the attacker's neck, the force of the impact driving him to the ground.

Where the heck had he come from? A quick glance around told me what I'd feared. Matthias had torn a portal through the ether. Scores of demons funneled through the portal and, though the wolves were cutting through them quickly, we were still gravely outnumbered.

Anger poured through my veins, and I rose into the air. Wind howled around me, mirroring the rage clouding my mind. Splintered rafters, chunks of mortar, and two demons flew through the air. I grinned with satisfaction.

Bricks whipped around us like meteors, pelting cars and houses, and mowing down monsters. Now where was Matthias?

Rhia shouted. A wolf was holding onto her by her belt and guarding her from the flying shrapnel with his body.

Panic tore through me. I was losing control. In the past, Damian's presence had always calmed me.

Closing my eyes, I focused on his face and the way his signature wrapped around me when we were close. My anger spiked, but then calmed, and the noise around me quieted.

"Nice work, Neve, but next time, direct the windstorm at your target, would ya?" Rhia shouted.

I opened my eyes. She'd climbed to her feet, and despite her disheveled hair, she was punching another demon in the face. *Badass bitch.*

Frantically searching for Matthias, I blasted a gust of wind toward a demon who materialized behind Rhia. The eddy slammed him backward, and he crashed into a pile of debris, impaled on a splintered door frame.

The cold whispers of an incantation dug into my bones, and I snapped my head up.

Matthias.

His eyes flashed with delight as he recited the spell. He held the bottle with both hands.

The words of the spell drained my power and wound around my throat like a garrot, strangling me. Agony cascaded through my body as he tore my freedom from me. I dropped to my knees.

This was not happening.

I could not let it.

Damian

The fluorescent light buzzed overhead as I rammed my knuckles into the demon's nose. It shattered with a sickening crunch.

The warehouse had been abandoned a few years ago due to structural damage. Most of the windows were blown out, and a large crack snaked across the building's western wall.

"Where is Matthias?" My voice echoed through the empty space.

The demon's head lolled to the side, a trickle of blood seeping out of his right nostril. He looked up at me with those black, soulless eyes and cracked a grin. "Close, angel. *Close.*"

I growled and shook out my hand. My men had managed to track down two of Matthias's demons and brought them to the warehouse for questioning. After some grisly work, I'd gotten a few answers out of the first, but nothing substantial.

Matthias was keeping his cards close to his chest, and his minions barely knew their own roles in the plan. I had to figure out his next move before he got the jump on us. Again.

Frustration raged in my heart. I knew Matthias was planning something—I knew him all too well. We'd been as close as brothers once and fought side by side against the Watchers, an order of Angels that were supposed to watch over the earth.

But *watch* was all they did. They had extremely powerful magic, but seldom acted, not wishing to interfere with the fate of the world.

I'd been one of them once. But eventually, I couldn't take their arrogance and callous dispassion any longer, and I'd rebelled. For a long time, there'd been a price on my head.

I'd betrayed the angels and joined Matthias. Now, he'd betrayed me.

Maybe it was fitting. Maybe it was what I deserved in the end. But Neve certainly didn't deserve to be tied up in my mess.

I shook my head, knowing the truth. For as many

things as I'd mess up, this wasn't about me or my history with Matthias.

He was after something much, much bigger.

Neve and her genie powers were at the center of his plans. I was just an inconvenient problem to be ignored while he hunted *her*. I'd do anything to stop him from getting to her. I just had to find an opening.

Wrapping my hand around the demon's throat, I pushed my cold magic into him. He began to shake and shiver. "I will turn you into a block of ice, if you don't tell me where Matthias is and what he's planning."

The devil just cackled through chattering teeth. "Go ahead and kill me, *fallen*. I'll just come back from hell to haunt you again and again."

I growled and shoved the chair and devil over backwards. "Fine. If that's all you've got for me, we're done here."

I tossed one of my men a pair of magicuffs. "Put those on him and sink him in the lake."

Fear flashed across the demon's face, and he tugged against the ropes that bound his wrists to the chair. With his magic restrained by the cuffs, he wouldn't return to the underworld to regenerate when he died. He'd be stuck at the bottom of the lake, somewhere between the clutches of life and death.

I had no pity for him.

I grabbed the rag from the back of the vacant metal

chair and wiped my bloodied knuckles. The skin had already knit itself together, but the bones still throbbed.

I flexed my fists. It had been a week since I'd been in the ring, and I needed to blow off some steam. Clear my head and get control. I hadn't seen Neve for two days, but she bombarded my thoughts, her magic relentlessly tugging on my dragon senses like a magnetic force. If it pulled any harder, I was bound to snap.

I couldn't change what I was—a FireSoul— but I'd considered asking Neve to wish away my magic cravings. I knew it was possible because I'd had the djinn do it once before. It would certainly lessen my cravings, but I'd lose much of my power in the process.

The dragon within roared in protest.

No.

I couldn't afford that with Matthias on our heels. Maybe once we'd defeated him.

The demon laughed behind me. "You're thinking of the genie woman, aren't you?"

Beating this fuck might help me focus.

Leaning his head back, the demon closed his eyes and inhaled deeply, his nostrils flaring. "You want to drink her in, take everything." He lowered his gaze to mine and sneered. "I don't blame you, FireSoul."

I growled, but the demon was right.

My cravings had grown since Neve had transitioned to a full djinn. Anger and guilt punched me in my gut.

She'd done it to save me, and now I was drawn to her magic like a moth to a flame.

In the past, my craving for power had grown so strong that nothing could stop me from taking what I wanted. I'd killed indiscriminately.

I couldn't stomach the idea of losing control and hurting Neve. Every part of my heart screamed that it wasn't possible, but my past whispered that it was.

My past was proof. It would only be a matter of time.

The best thing I could do to protect her was to stay away and hunt down Matthias. To do that, I needed to rein in the dragon.

"It won't be long now. He's coming for her." The demon was taunting me, hoping to buy time, but I'd take the bait.

"What do you mean?" I crossed the distance and lowered my gaze to his. "Where is he exactly?"

"That depends. What time is it?"

A low rumble built in my chest, and flames cascaded down my arms. "Where?"

My voice boomed through the empty space, and the demon grimaced. "Don't know. Only that he's planning to catch her today."

I glanced at Tommy. "See that this bastard is on the bottom of Lake Michigan."

Slipping a pair of magicuffs into my back pocket, I turned and exited the warehouse. The demon's curses echoed behind me as I pulled out my phone. Glancing down at the screen, it rang. *Alastair.* Just the man I was going to call.

"What is it?" I answered.

"Malek, we've got a situation. Matthias and his gang of demons are here. We need backup."

A growl slipped from my throat. "Where are you?"

"A burnt down house at 6300 Stone Haven."

They'd gone to Matthias's house. *Gods damn it.*

"Protect Miss Cross, whatever it takes." Ending the call, I slipped the phone into my pocket.

There was no time do drive. Unleashing my wings, I launched into the air. Flight in Magic Side was prohibited, but I wasn't one to be bound by the Order's laws.

Soaring over the old warehouses in the Dockside Dens, I narrowed my eyes on the Gaslight District.

I'm coming for you, Matthias.

3

Neve

My vision blurred from the pain. I clutched my stomach, gasping for air. My insides felt like they were being wrung through a juicer, and the binding spell clenched around me, draining my magic.

Shithead Matthias.

He hovered in the air on black wings, just out of reach of the wolves, as if taunting them. All the while, he recited the damn binding spell. The same one he'd taught me to use, the one I'd trapped the djinn with almost three weeks ago.

Each word drew the noose tighter, and gods did it hurt.

"Neve!" Rhia grabbed my shoulders, pulling me upright.

My muscles cramped at the sudden movement, and I screamed.

"I'm going to slow down time so we can get the hell out of here," she said.

I nodded, blinking rapidly to clear my vision. A demon lurched toward us, then—as if Rhiannon had hit pause on a TV remote—his movements slowed to a halt. The agony inside me lessened as Matthias's chant paused.

"Come on! I can't hold it for long." Rhiannon tugged on my arm. All the shifters and demons around us were frozen in place.

"Wait." I turned to Matthias. Now was my chance to nab the POS. I reached for the pair of magicuffs on my holster, but my fingers came up short. Damn I'd left them on the front seat of the car.

Did I have time to grab them?

The movements of the demons and shifters began to quicken. Still slow like molasses, but definitely faster. Rhia's hold on time was slipping.

Guess I'd have to restrain Matthias the hard way.

I wasn't sure I could fly, so I'd have to knock him out of the sky.

I leapt over a pile of bricks and closed the distance with him, drawing my magic to my fists. But instead of an avalanche, it felt like a trickle. The binding spell was bleeding my power.

"Incoming!" Rhia screamed, and time returned.

Confusion crossed Matthias's face as the last word he'd spoken drawled out of his throat. With the flick of my wrists, I blasted him head over heels with a burst of wind. That tiny release of magic left me drained, but he landed on his ass in the middle of the bricks with a satisfying crunch.

Panic rose in my throat, so I latched onto the anger coursing through me. It gave me strength.

Matthias scrambled for the khanjar as I crossed toward him. I pinned him in place with a steady stream of air and sucked the breath from his lungs with a single inhale. His face contorted, and he clutched at his throat.

My anger fueled my magic, so I fed it, focusing on all the shit he'd done to me.

Everything around me quieted—the screams and growls, the crashing—it all faded away. Everything but my rage for Matthias.

Gods, I could kill him right now. And I wanted to. More than anything else in the world, I wanted to snuff the life right out of him.

No.

The whisper of reason bounced off the walls of my conscious mind. I'd made a blood oath with Zara to bring Matthias in alive. The consequences of breaking the oath didn't bother me as much as breaking the promise.

But I wanted to kill him *so bad*. Make him suffer for the pain he'd caused me and my friends.

No.

Fury vibrated through my body, and I clutched my head.

My mind felt like it was going to calve in two. Squeezing my eyes shut, I struggled to get control over my raging thoughts. My magic flickered out, and my hold over Matthias faltered.

A modicum of relief returned, and I opened my eyes, meeting Matthias's gaze. Khanjar in hand, he launched back into the sky and began the incantation again.

You should have killed him when you had the chance.

I howled as my muscles spasmed and the spell's stranglehold returned. My strength left me like a tidal wave, and my legs shook, unable to hold me upright.

I had to escape.

I leapt into the air, trying to call the wind. Claws dug into my side as a demon caught me and slammed me down into the rubble.

"Kill him, Rhia." I forced the words from my throat. I'd break my promise to Zara if it meant not being bound to her father.

Tears lined my eyes as the shouts and growls around me intensified. A wolf leapt over my body in a blur, aiming for Matthias. He must have missed because the vice on my body hadn't lessened, and my magic felt all but depleted.

A translucent collar started forming around my neck

as I tried to scramble to my knees, but a savage claw thrust me down. It was almost over.

Closing my eyes, I swore I felt a cool, ocean breeze caress my cheek. The smell of pine wafted through my nose. I was losing it. My mind was latching on to memories, like what happened right before you died. Supposedly.

I'd take it.

A fireball exploded beside me, and Matthias screamed. The spell broke.

I tried to get up but had no strength.

A large, winged shadow loomed above me, blocking the sun's rays from warming my face.

Matthias?

I scuttled backwards, but two strong arms scooped me up, cradling me against a solid chest. Warmth cascaded through me, and the smell of pine and sandalwood lulled my nerves.

My gaze fixated on two brilliant green eyes. Damian. Worry and anger streaked across his face as he flew across the street.

Having been momentarily stunned by Damian's angelic beauty and euphoric signature, I arched my neck around, searching the wreckage.

Where was Rhiannon? Where was Matthias?

My best friend was at the center of a scene of pure chaos. Rhiannon threw her bolas at a demon, then lunged at another, driving a blade into its leg. The shifters were all in wolf form, tearing off the limbs of several pinned demons and corralling others.

And Matthias. He climbed to his feet, eyes searching the ground.

"Stay here," Damian rumbled, setting me on the ground beside the silver cruiser before he launched into the air.

The black feathers on his wings glinted in the sun, and I couldn't help but be awed by his magnificence. And gods damned beauty.

My traitorous thoughts had returned.

I climbed to my feet and stumbled. I was utterly drained, like a wilted daisy, or a shriveled French fry. The bastard Matthias must have nearly finished the binding spell.

Fates, what would have happened if he had? Would I be powerless? It sure felt that way, but the other genies Matthias had bound—the marid, the djinn, and the efreet— still had their magic afterward.

I wiped my clammy palms on my jeans. There was so much I didn't understand about being a genie.

I needed answers. *Fast.*

My life and freedom depended on it.

Damian

Bricks and mortar crunched as I landed behind Matthias.

He turned, dismissing Neve's old khanjar into the ether as my fist slammed into his jaw. His head snapped to the side, and he stumbled before meeting my gaze.

"Meddling with my plans yet again, brother. When will you learn that we're an even match?" He spat a mouthful of blood onto the rubble.

"With your two genies and demon army, I'd say we might come close to even. Why don't you step away from your bodyguards and fight me like a man, you fucking coward?"

Matthias's eyes darted over my shoulder, and he grinned. "You mean we could end this rivalry with a go in the ring? Why didn't you say so sooner?"

Dismissing my wings, I surged forward, striking him in the chest with my fist. I grinned at the crack of his ribs. He stumbled back but managed to stay upright, clutching his side.

He drew his fists together and moved slowly, preparing to attack. Glancing over my shoulder again, he surged forward like a viper. A black blade flashed in one of his hands as I blocked the punch from the other. The cursed weapon sank into my torso and then twisted.

Bastard always played dirty.

Biting pain throbbed in my side, but I kneed Matthias in the groin and brought my elbow down with a crack into his back. His knees buckled and he slumped to my feet.

Grabbing the scruff of his neck, I pulled his head back so I could look at his face. His lips moved in a whisper, and every muscle in me spasmed. A spell or a curse.

"Two can play at this game," I growled, unleashing a waterfall of flames down my arm. They enveloped Matthias's neck, and he screamed and twisted, but my grip was iron.

The stink of scalded flesh burned my lungs. Reaching around, I grabbed the magicuffs in my pants and slammed one onto his wrist. "This ends today."

Neve's scream tore through my chest.

I whipped around, searching. Two demons had a hold of her arms, but she managed to kick the third in the face. She—

A burning pain stabbed me in the back.

Blood trickled down my side from the wound, and fury rocketed through me. The flames followed, shooting forth from my body like a raging fire.

Matthias howled in pain.

Neve's eyes locked onto mine, and she gasped as one of the demons injected her with a needle. Her head slumped forward, and her legs slackened. They slid her in the back of the SUV.

I roared—a guttural rumble that ripped free of my chest.

"You'll have to choose," Matthias said between shrieks. "Me or her."

The SUV's engine revved.

"Fuck!" I slammed the other cuff around Matthias's wrist, shoved him to the ground, and launched into the sky. My wings caught me and lifted me above a demon who raked his claws through the air, trying to latch onto my leg.

"Get her," Rhiannon shouted from below. "I'm right behind you!"

She'd broken the neck of the demon who'd tackled her and was sprinting toward the street.

The black SUV's tires screamed as it peeled away from the curve and raced down the street, weaving side to side. I raced through the air.

They'd drugged Neve and hijacked the shifters' ride. Was this Matthias's backup plan, or had he calculated this all along?

I growled and surged ahead of the SUV, landing in the middle of the street as the vehicle squealed around the corner. The demon behind the wheel gunned the engine, driving straight for me. Narrowing my eyes, I spotted Neve in the back seat with the outlines of a seatbelt secured across her chest.

Planting my feet on the pavement, I called forth my magic, feeling the flames, and ice, and darkness twining down my arms.

Fuckers chose the wrong angel to play chicken with.

Rhiannon leapt through a hedge and appeared on the sidewalk. She looked between me and the oncoming car and nodded. "Do it!"

What in the gods' names was she planning to do?

Wind rushed into me as the car closed in. A second before impact, I stepped forward, releasing a font of energy into the hood. The grill dented in with a deafening crash, and the car lifted into the air above me, its back end rising.

I prepared another pulse of energy to envelope the car and slow its spin, but...everything slowed. The gods damned car had stopped mid spin and was floating upside down.

"Stop twiddling your thumbs, Malek! I can't hold time forever."

Holy shit. She'd done this trick in the djinn palace.

Leaping into the air, I grabbed hold of the rack on the roof and pulled myself up. Standing on the running board, I wrenched the door open, tearing it from its hinges. As it left my hand it started floating, falling downward in slow motion.

Neve was unconscious, slumped forward against her seatbelt, her breathing shallow.

"Hurry it up, man!" Rhiannon shouted.

I unclicked the seatbelt and caught Neve as she fell into my arms. Cradling her to my chest, I leapt out of the car backward, just as Rhiannon's hold over time ended.

Unfurling my wings, I soared up as the SUV, no

longer inhibited by Rhiannon's time-stop, flipped through the air, and crashed into the street. Sparks flew across the pavement as the vehicle slid to a stop.

"Holy-mother-of-gods-yeah!" Rhiannon fist pumped the air.

I glanced down at Neve whose cheek was pressed against my shoulder. Heat coursed between us where our bodies touched, and a deep ache lodged in my chest. Her magic signature danced across my nerve endings, and my pulse quickened.

Get yourself under control, fool.

4

Neve

Wincing at the pain, I snuggled into the warm, pillowy goodness that smelled of lavender and herbs. Every muscle in my body ached like it had been stretched beyond its limit. But the sheets were silky and crisp. Freshly laundered.

Sighing, I let drowsiness and the smell of the ocean and sandalwood soothe my—

My eyelids shot open, and I gripped the comforter cocooning me. Holding my breath, I peered over the peaks of the white duvet until my eyes locked onto Damian's forest green eyes.

He was seated on a chair at the far end of the room with a smirk stuck on his face. "I like the way you look in my bed."

His bed? Panic flared, and I looked under the sheets.

Oh, thank fates, I wasn't naked.

But why was I here? And *oh my gods*, I was in my underwear and an oversized T-shirt that definitely wasn't mine.

I couldn't remember anything. What had happened?

My cheeks burned and I sank under the covers before releasing my breath. Did we...?

I was going to curse the fates if we had, and I'd forgotten. Because the memory of Damian's head between my thighs on the beach in Apollonia Parva was something I never wanted to forget.

Damian chuckled softly and cleared his throat. "Your virtue is safe. You're wearing my shirt, but that was Rhiannon's doing."

The traitorous part of me sulked. Time to face the music.

I sat up gingerly and glared at him, my head a little cloudy. He'd changed since Matthias's house. Blue jeans and a black shirt that hugged his chest in ways that should have been illegal.

The memory of Matthias made me wince, but Damian sitting on that chair with his legs spread and that sexy look on his face made my insides tingle in all the right ways.

One ticket for the Damian ride, please.

My gods, my mind must have pranced away on holiday, leaving my rather untrustworthy body in charge.

I rubbed my face, hoping to clear the vision of

Damian that was seared into my neurons. I glanced around the room. "What happened?"

Nope, the vision was still there.

"Matthias attacked you, then his demons drugged and kidnapped you...or tried to."

So that explained why everything felt fuzzy. I stole a glance at Damian. The smugness from earlier was replaced with concern. His eyes darkened and he stood, and just like that, the stone-cold angel had returned.

So much for that ride.

Man, those drugs were really doing a number on me.

I had to ask, though I dreaded the response. "Did we get Matthias?"

Damian scowled. "No. He got away."

Despair sank into my soul. This would happen again and again and again. Until he caught me. Or we killed him.

Worry crept into my chest, and all my muscles tensed. "Where's Rhia? Is she okay?"

"She insisted on picking up hot dogs and gelato." Damian paused and frowned. "Why she would do that is beyond reason. But she refused to budge, so I sent her with my security detail. She's safe."

Relief poured through me, and I forced back a knowing smile. "Wait, you sent her with the shifters?"

"Yes. Why?"

I smiled, and my eyes watered from the strain. "Oh, she'll be just fine, but they won't."

"Speak of the devil." Damian glanced out the window. "I'll check on my men."

I laughed as Damian left the room, then I sank into the pillow-top goodness.

For the moment, I was safe.

Shit had been bad, and was bound to get worse, so I was going to savor these few minutes of happiness—drug induced or not. I pulled the duvet over my head and breathed in the clean-sheet perfume that was laced with hints of Damian.

I must have dozed because I jumped when Rhiannon barged through the door.

"Oh fates, sorry! Damian said you were awake." Rhia clutched Sammy's signature white-and-red takeout bag and a melting cup of lemon gelato. "How are you feeling?"

"I'm starving." Wincing, I scooted upright and gave her my best grabby hands. "You are my savior, Rhia."

I dug into the gelato first, and she plopped the bag of dogs onto my lap. "Oh my gods, this is so good," I moaned.

Rhia grinned. "Other than your gelato-gasm, how else do you feel?"

"Drugged out of my mind, and like my body was run over by a truck." Having shoveled the three scoops of gelato down my throat, I tilted my head back and poured the last dribbles of lemony goodness into my mouth.

"Well, that's not far from what happened."

"Wait, what?"

Her eyes rounded. "What do you remember?"

My mind was beginning to work again. Slightly. "I mean, I remember Matthias and Damian swooping in. But after that, it's blank."

"That's a blessing. But damn—" She leaned close and glanced back at the open door. "Damian was badass. When the devils took you, he went nuts. He chased you down and flipped the freaking car with his bare hands."

I blinked twice and sunk my teeth into my Chicago dog, another moan escaping my lips. "So that's why I feel like roadkill."

I didn't quite understand what Rhiannon was describing, but man was this dog good. Rhia had asked for extra magic peppers, too. The bomb.

A knock on the door stole my attention away from my lunch.

Damian stood in the doorway with a stern expression. "Once you finish up, we should all talk. There's an extra toothbrush in my bathroom and feel free to use the shower."

I nodded, my mouth stuffed like a chipmunk.

Damian disappeared from the doorway, and Rhia rubbed a smudge of ketchup off my chin.

I blanched. "Crap. I'm a mess, aren't I?"

Rhia grinned and took my measure. "You'd better climb into Damian's shower. Scrub off all that filth."

Damian's shower? Heat flashed through me. "Wait a sec. When you say filth, are you talking literally or figuratively?"

She hopped up and unzipped a weekender bag that had mysteriously appeared at the foot of the bed. "Both. I picked up some of your clothes. Damian's shirt looks good, but the way he keeps staring at you in it is making me uncomfortable."

"You, uncomfortable? Unlikely." I grinned as she handed me a neatly stacked pile of clothes. Black jeans, a cream sweater, and—a thong! "Seriously, Rhia? Couldn't you have brought me a pair of granny panties?"

She chuckled. "Sorry, I grabbed the first pair I saw."

"Why are you so okay with this?" I gestured around the room with a sweeping circle motion.

"With Damian you mean? Look, I know he's a scary beast who may or may not want to eat your magic, but after seeing him in action today, I know two things for certain. One, he's crazy about you. And two, he's the only one here"—she did a replay of my sweeping circle gesture— "who can protect you. So, I'm giving him a chance, but I'm also keeping my eye on him."

"Uh huh, and the shifters, am I right?"

She strutted to the door and turned back with a wink. "Girl, you know me too well. Holler if you need me."

I smiled and hobbled to the bathroom. Boy, was I stiff. I needed a stiff cocktail. Not to mention a stiff—

Holy heck.

I needed to purge these dirty thoughts from my mind, ASAP.

Unsurprisingly, the bathroom was big. A huge white soaking tub, which I could use right now, a ginormous walk-in shower lined with river pebbles, and...a double vanity?

Did Damian entertain regularly?

Brushing aside the irritation that simmered in my chest, I stripped and flipped on the hot water.

"Instant hot water?" I murmured. And a rain showerhead. The hot water in my old apartment flowed like a trickle, tended to sputter, and sometimes smelled like the lake.

The shower felt divine, but I made quick work of it. As much as slipping away from reality was amazing with a capital A, we had shit to do.

Like finding Matthias and figuring out what it meant to be a genie.

The drugs that Matthias's demons had hit me with had clearly worn off, because by the time I stepped out of the shower, I felt the weight of the world on my shoulders.

Shit was grim.

I stared at myself in the mirror as I brushed my teeth with the spare toothbrush Damian had left me—on *his* side of the vanity judging from the other toothbrush beside it.

I'd take that as a win.

Five minutes later, I strolled into the living room fresh as a daisy.

My jaw dropped. Rhiannon was perched on the couch surrounded by four shifters. Correction. Four *hot* shifters, and they were totally digging her.

I rolled my eyes and caught Damian's gaze in the process.

He approached me carefully. Maintaining a distance, his eyes roamed over my body, stoking a deep heat inside of me. "Feeling better?"

"Yes. Much." The words lodged in my throat, but I forced them out, my voice sounding a little too high pitched.

Rhia materialized by my side and squeezed my shoulder. "You're looking refreshed."

"Should we get down to business?" Damian gestured toward the study.

We followed him in and sat side-by-side on a couch in front of the low coffee table. Damian closed the door and took a seat by his desk at the far end of the room.

Was he really that affected by my proximity?

If so, fates, were we in trouble.

Damian flexed his fist absently. "That was far too close."

I shut my eyes for a second. The memory of

Matthias's magic wrapping around my throat washed away the warm sense of security I'd had lounging in Damian's bed. Matthias was out there. Hunting me.

A shudder ran down my spine. "You can say that again."

"We need a plan to get this fucker once and for all," Rhia hissed. "Neve wasn't the only target. I texted Gretchen earlier to let her know what happened, and she just got back to me. Apparently, there's been an influx of demons since this last night. The Order managed to catch a couple of them, but not before another operative was kidnapped."

"Another? When did this happen, and why?"

Rhia shrugged. "Apparently, around the same time they came after you. I don't know why."

A low growl escaped Damian's throat. "He's looking for information and trying to size up the Order's weaknesses."

I shot him a piercing look. "How do you know that?"

"Because I fought at his side for a long time. And because I've been doing the same thing."

"What?" Rhia exclaimed.

"There've been a few rogue demons in town, scouting for info. I had my people pick them up, and we've been asking questions—the hard way." He fixed me with a long gaze, and my stomach churned.

It was easy to forget that Damian had another life in which he was a ruthless crime lord who wouldn't blink an eye at grabbing someone off the street and brutally squeezing them for information.

It was horrible, but I was somehow okay with it. And that made me sick.

I rubbed my eyes. "I'm so tired of always reacting, of running away from this *asshole*. Matthias ambushed us at his house, at Apollonia, at the Archives, at Helwan. We need to take this battle to him. Hit him in the nuts. Take him down when he's not expecting it."

"Great, but how?" Rhia asked. "He's clearly tracking us, but we have no idea where he is, or what he's up to."

I recalled the realm I'd seen through Damian's memories, and irritation rippled through me. "I assume he's holed up in his tower in the Realm of Chaos, making plans to invade the city. Either there or waiting in the driveway to nab me the moment we step outside."

"You're safe here," Damian said quietly. "Matthias is nowhere near Magic Side. I can't feel him with my dragon sense. He's probably not even on this plane."

I shuddered at the reminder of what Damian was. His *FireSoul* magic allowed him to find the things he wanted. And judging by the fire in his eyes and the tension in his body, I was pretty sure he wanted to rip Matthias's heart out and was concentrating very hard on that image.

My heartbeat accelerated for no apparent reason.

Rhia scowled. "So, what do we do? Try to lure him out of his fortress? Wait for him to attack again?"

"Absolutely not," Damian said, his tone cold. "We tried that at Apollonia, and he ended up getting the jump on us. We need to turn the tables. I have an idea, but it will be risky."

I leaned forward. "What?"

"There's a backdoor to the fortress. Before Matthias transported the Searing Citadel to the Realm of Chaos, I explored the tower and found a teleportation circle. I took pictures. We could use that information to make a similar portal here that would connect to the one in the tower. A gateway inside."

I recalled the photos Damian had shown Lily and me of the runes last week. "Won't it be guarded?"

"Yes, but Matthias has no idea that we know it exists. So, we might get lucky. We take a small team, sneak in and take the bastard out at his desk before he knows what hit him. It's the one place he probably thinks he's safe, and that makes him vulnerable."

I stood and started pacing. "Before we run off to the citadel, we need to talk about the elephant in the room. I have an insane amount of power that is inextricably linked to emotions that I have little control over. The longer I can't control my magic, the easier it will be for Matthias to bind me. I'm a liability."

"True. That's why you should stay here. I'll take a team in. Trained killers. Quiet and fast."

I spun and locked Damian with a piercing stare. "Absolutely not. I am going with. Matthias is mine. I'm sorry, but the truth is, I'm the only one with the strength to defeat him."

Damian tensed, and flames danced in his eyes. "Yet he's got the power to drain your magic and bind you. We got very lucky this time."

"That's why our first priority should be figuring out how to make sure I can control my magic and avoid his binding spell. If you and your team of cutthroats fail, then he'll come straight for me, and we'll be in an even shittier situation."

"She's right," Rhia said. "We need to find a way for Neve to resist the binding spell."

"But how?" Damian asked, unconvinced. "You'd need to find someone with magic like yours."

"Well, we're shit out of luck because the only djinn I know is a psychopath who wants to tear my limbs off. That's a hard pass." I plopped down onto the way-too-firm couch.

"What about the marid king?" Damian asked.

Rhia rested her elbows on her knees and turned to me. "You mean the father of that half water genie you guys rescued from the Searing Citadel? Didn't he banish Damian?"

I nodded but frowned. "That won't be enough. I spoke with him before I returned. The marid king has been a genie his entire life. He doesn't know what I'm going through. Besides, he has mastery over the oceans. *I* am from the Realm of Air. Quite a bit of a difference."

Rhia and Damian were silent.

"I need a djinn. Someone who is related to me." I sighed. What I needed was my family.

An idea sparked in my mind. The way the djinn had spoken about them to me suggested they were out there.

"That's it!" I whispered, almost under my breath.

I just needed to find them. And now I had the power to do so.

My eyes met Damian's piercing gaze. "I need you to make a wish. My parents might still be alive, and if so, I must speak with them. They might be able to teach me something about my powers. I've looked for them before, but with a wish..."

His jaw clenched and his eyes narrowed. "You know that's too dangerous, Neve. I won't do it."

Irritation prickled my skin. "Damn it, Damian. Your wish got us into this mess. Now you've got to help me fix this. This could solve one of our biggest problems. I can't control my magic. You of all people know what that means."

My words cut through the air, and Damian went rigid. Regret and guilt flickered in his eyes. The silence between us grew, and I could feel Rhia's unease wafting through the room.

I fixed him with a glare. "My magic is our best weapon against Matthias. If I can't use it, we're fighting with one hand behind our back. We need to use my powers to our advantage."

He sighed. "Fine. You're right. We need to take advantage of your powers. However, we also need to be careful. I have a couple stipulations."

I scowled.

"One, I'm only going to wish that you can speak to your parents. I don't trust us to wish for anything more than that. Don't try to go to them. You don't know what situation they could be in. And don't summon them here. We don't understand your powers or how they work yet, and the consequences could be disastrous. Just find out where they are, what they can tell us about your magic, and how to use a binding spell. Deal?"

My *parents*.

I couldn't believe this was happening. "Deal."

"Once we figure out how to control your magic and break the binding spell, we recruit a team to infiltrate the citadel and take Matthias out. The longer we delay, the greater the risk to you and Magic Side."

Relief and excitement fluttered in my chest. I was going to be reunited with my parents. I'd always assumed they were dead, but the djinn's words in the Realm of Air suggested they were out there. *Alive.* And now I was going to find them.

"Deal." I grinned ear to ear.

The day was finally looking up.

5

Neve

Five minutes later, I was sitting face to face with Damian. His eyes burned into me, and it took every ounce of willpower to ignore the way his closeness sent shivers racing up my thighs.

I thought my body and I had come to terms with this. Apparently not.

How had it come to this? A genie crushing on a fallen angel that might kill her. My cheeks burned with embarrassment.

I closed my eyes and pushed him out of my mind. I had to focus on controlling my magic.

When Damian had wished for me to heal him, I'd seen a thousand possibilities. I'd panicked and chosen one at random where he was whole again. I'd gotten lucky.

If I could control my choice, I could get exactly what I wanted. In legends, genies always twisted wishes. Damian had said as much about the djinn. Maybe, if I focused, I could twist the wish to my advantage.

I took a deep breath, letting the air calm my mind, and I opened my eyes.

"Okay. I'm ready," I said in a shaky voice. I wasn't afraid to see my parents again, just feeling the unease of the butterflies doing somersaults in my stomach.

Damian locked me with those piercing green eyes. "Are you sure about this?"

"Abso-freaking-lutely." I winked at Rhiannon who was looking pale. In fact, both her and Damian looked pale. "I'll be *fine* you guys."

If not, I'd figure it out as I went. No chance in hell I'd miss the chance to find out where my parents were.

"Alright, let's give it a whirl," Rhia said, glancing at Damian, whose gaze never left mine.

He ground his teeth but nodded. "Fine. But promise me you'll stay focused and be careful."

I handed Rhia my phone for safe keeping. "I promise."

Lie.

I'd do whatever it took to find my parents. Damian had no idea how long I'd prayed for this moment.

I'd always assumed they were dead, but sometimes, I had dreams where they were still alive. Dreams where their disappearance had just been a big misunder-standing.

Maybe it was.

"All right." He took my hands. "Then genie, I wish for you to find your parents so that you may speak to them."

His words drifted through the air, almost as if Rhia had slowed time. Then they hit me like a freight train. I gasped and arched my back as a thousand tiny fires came to life inside of me.

My magic was back.

My vision blurred to black, and I blinked, opening my eyes to the cosmos. Rhia and Damian were gone. The apartment was gone. I was floating in a black abyss surrounded by flickering lights; each was a doorway of possibility. Endless opportunities. My mind homed in on one, and I turned, focusing my burning gaze on it. There, behind a glowing door, were my parents.

My heart seized, and I reached out. They were so close I could touch them. And why not? My power was infinite.

I reached forward, touching the light that emanated from the portal to my parents. Warmth flooded me, and then a violent force latched onto my wrist, tugging me through a worm hole.

My body spun through the darkness as the invisible force pulled me in every direction, like a rollercoaster from hell. I screamed, but my voice was drowned out in the vacuum of space.

Fear consumed me, and I hugged my knees, praying to the gods that wherever I ended up, it was in one piece.

Fates, what have I done?

Damian

Neve disappeared in a burst of wind.

The air tore from my lungs as the invisible thread that linked us together snapped, like a high-tension cable, a sucker punch to the gut.

The world spun.

She's gone.

"What happened? Where did she go?" Rhiannon shoved me.

I shook my head, trying to clear my thoughts. "I have no idea, but I can't sense her. She's somewhere far."

"Shit!" Rhiannon snapped. "The wish was clear, you said it perfectly."

I had. Against my better judgement, and once again, it had come back to haunt me. Worry and frustration churned in my veins, like an angry sea breaking against the shore. I should have stood my ground. Whatever happened from here on out was the fault of my weakness.

I had to find her. *Fast.*

I racked my brain. "I wished that she could speak with her parents again, that was it. We reasoned it out."

Rhiannon paced the room, face flushed. "Fates, what if her parents are dead? What if the only way to speak to them was by her dying and going to an afterlife!"

My stomach knotted. I hadn't thought of that. Gods, what had I done? Why was I so arrogant in the face of magic I didn't understand?

She spun on me. "We knew she couldn't control her magic. This is our fault."

I set my jaw. "We'll get her back."

"How can you say that? We have no idea where she is."

"We'll get her back. If I have to fight my way through the entire fucking netherworld, I'll do it."

She glared, but finally, the tension drained from her shoulders. "Wherever you're going, I'm coming with."

"I wouldn't expect anything else. We need a seer. Lily DuVoir knows Neve already, which will make it easier for her to find her." I didn't wait for a response. I dug my keys out and strode to the car.

After a shocked moment, Rhiannon hurried after.

She hopped in beside me and slammed the door. "How far can you sense Neve with, well, whatever it is you've got?"

I turned the ignition. "My dragon sense. I'm not sure what the range is... miles for certain, and her pull is incredibly strong. She hasn't been out of my range since I returned from exploring the Searing Citadel."

"Could you feel her if she were in Guild City? How about on the other side of the world?"

I shook my head as we roared down the Midway toward the Dockside Dens. "I have no idea."

Rhiannon sunk into her seat, her expression grim. I tightened my grip on the wheel, my knuckles turning white. "Call Lily. You have her number I assume? Let her know we're on our way."

She nodded and put the call through. I pulled out my cell and speed dialed the Dockside boss. "Alastair, it's Damian. I'm headed into Dockside to see Lily. I just wanted to give you a heads-up. No surprises."

He consented, and I hung up. Dockside was run by a shifter pack, and they were damned territorial. It was all too easy to ruffle their fur. It was always best to give the alpha a heads-up—a courtesy amongst rivals. I'd hired some of Alastair's wolves to protect Neve, but that was only possible because the alpha had owed me debt.

Ten minutes later, I pulled to a halt in front of Lily DuVoir's apartment building—an old redbrick structure with an Art Deco tower.

I nodded to some shifters stationed across the way as we got out of the car. They were probably expecting us by now. I found Lily's button on the call box under *Madam DuVoir—mysteries and curses divined.* The button made an ear-grating buzz as I pressed it. After a few seconds, the door unlocked with an electric clack, and we headed inside.

Lily DuVoir was waiting at the top of the landing. She had dark, curly hair and a timeless youth to her. Anxiety uncharacteristically tugged at the edges of her expression.

"What's happened to Neve?" She spoke with a slight French accent that turned up the corners of her words.

We explained the situation as Lily led us into her sitting room. While she listened, she pulled a small table into the center of the room and set up three mismatched vintage chairs. "Sit, sit."

I pulled a chair back for Rhiannon and sat down beside her.

Lily flicked her wrist, and the heavy drapes slid closed, and the lights dimmed. "I'm more of a specialist in curses. I will look, but I make no guarantees. Do you have anything of hers?"

"Not now. We could—"

"No matter. I know her, which makes things easier— though even a small trinket would have helped." Lily placed a crystal ball on the table and took the last remaining chair. "Join hands."

Rhiannon took my hand without a second thought. Lily placed her fingers in my palm and quickly raised a quizzical eyebrow. *How much could she read through that touch?*

It didn't matter. Even if she discovered I was a Fire-Soul, I had to get Neve back.

Lily closed her eyes and rolled her head side to side. "Good, now close your eyes and concentrate on Neve. And for heaven's sake, keep your mouths shut while I'm working. Any yammering, and we'll have to start over."

I closed my eyes. Rhiannon's grip tightened as Lily's magic swirled around us. Chicory and the taste of caramel. I pushed her signature out of my mind and focused on Neve.

The vibrant tint of her red hair, and the way it danced around her face even when there wasn't a breeze. The intricate pattern of the tattoos that wound around her arms and across her chest. The way she mouthed words when reading. The way her lips felt against mine. The way she tasted.

I reached out with my dragon sense but found only absence. The minutes dragged on.

Suddenly, Lily threw my hand down in exasperation. "I've got absolutely nothing."

My stomach twisted, and I opened my eyes. "What does that mean?"

"She's not on Earth, that's for sure. She might be in one of the netherworlds or hells, possibly in one of the planes. Wasn't her family from the Realm of Air?"

Rhiannon's eyes darted to mine, and she nodded. "Yes. Can you see that far?"

"No, that would require a specialized crystal ball or something connected to the planes."

I summoned the Atlas of the Planes from the ether and laid it on the table. "Would this help? It's an atlas of the Realms of Air, Earth, Fire, and Water."

I'd been meaning to give it to Neve. Since I'd stolen the efreet's magic and could planes-walk, I found that I could read it—though I hadn't tried to use it for travel yet.

A dark thought suddenly tugged at me. What the Atlas didn't have was a map of Matthias's Realm of Chaos. If Neve had been transported there...

I kept my worries to myself.

Lily eagerly opened the Atlas and flipped the large pages over. "They're blank."

"You have to be a planes-walker to see them. Currently, you're looking at Muqaddasī's notes on the Realm of Fire."

Lily pursed her lips. "Hmm. This might do."

She tossed her crystal ball onto her green couch with a surprising lack of concern. She positioned the book where the ball had been, leaving it open to the Realm of Fire.

She took our hands. "We try again."

I closed my eyes and focused on Neve, not just the woman I'd first met, but the djinn. Vibrating with power, tattoos glowing with white light. That's who she was now.

Neve's signature swirled in my mind. The heady scent of a lemon orchard and jasmine hedges. I could almost hear the echoing cry of sea birds. The feel of the wind eddied around me, and I tasted a rainstorm on the way. Her signature was like vertigo, like falling a thousand miles into the sky. By now, I knew it better than I knew my own.

Lily gasped and yanked her hand away. My eyes shot open. She flipped the page over and jabbed her finger down. "She's here. Where is it?"

I leaned over, and a lump formed in my throat.

"The Realm of Earth." I met Rhiannon's eyes. "Her contrary plane. Neve won't be able to planes-walk out, and her magic will be weak."

Rhiannon's pupils dilated. "What do we do?"

I clenched my fist. "We get her the fuck out of there, as fast as possible."

6

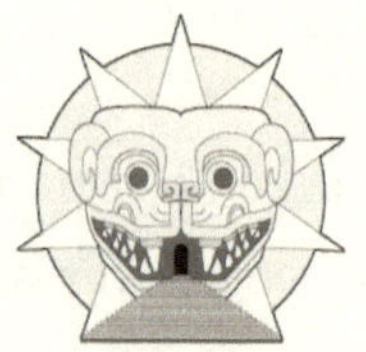

Neve

I felt like a lightning rod as unimaginable power surged through my body.

The ether ejected me into darkness, and gravel and flecks of rock cut into my palms and knees. Disoriented I tried to stand, but a wave of exhaustion churned through me, and I flopped over onto my ass.

Sucking in a sharp breath, I tasted dust, and my lungs rasped, burning as if they were closing in on themselves. Panic shot through my veins as my lungs tightened. There wasn't enough air.

I called on my magic but felt almost nothing. Fighting against hypoxia, I pulled a small breeze around me, so slight it barely stirred my hair, but it was enough. My lungs filled, and my breathing steadied.

Holy shit. What have I gotten myself into?

Damian had wished that I could speak to my parents, and now I was in some kind of cave. Were my parents here, too? I'd seen them in the ether and reached out to them before I was sucked in.

"Hello?" I whispered.

"Who's there?" A sharp male voice hissed back.

My heart stopped. I wasn't alone.

I tried to speak, but my chest seized up, and it came out as a croak. This was all too much to hope for.

"I thought I heard someone," the voice muttered.

"I did, too," a woman whispered.

Did I recognize that voice? My heart thundered, and I pulled my magic around me tightly, trying to calm my breathing.

Was it them? I had to know.

"My name is Nevaeh. I don't know where I am, and I'm not sure how I got here. I'm looking for my parents, Alain and Tinaya. Can you help me?"

Someone gasped, and a sob formed in my throat.

"Nevaeh?" the woman said.

"Quiet. It's a trap," the man said. "They're tormenting us again. Don't respond."

My body shook with emotion. "Mom? Dad? It's me," I choked out.

I heard nothing but the slightest sound of repressed breathing. They didn't believe me.

My muscles ached, so I rolled over and crawled forward. My eyes hadn't yet adjusted to the darkness, and my head collided with solid metal. A bite of pain shot across my scalp.

"Where am I?" I reached out and gripped a cold metal bar. A row of them. "I'm in some kind of cell. Are you prisoners? Do you have any light?"

Someone sucked in their breath. There was no response, though I could almost feel their words hanging in the air. They were afraid. I had to get them talking.

"I swear this isn't a trick. I'm a half-djinn with natural red hair and pale blue eyes. I planes-walked for the first time fifteen years ago and lost my parents. I grew up in an orphanage in Magic Side, Chicago. I remember my father reading to me, and my mother playing a guitar, or lute, or something like it."

The woman sobbed. "Nevaeh? Is it really you?"

"It can't be," the man whispered. "He must be playing with our minds. No one can get in or out of this place."

I bit my lip as tears ran down my cheeks. After all this time, they were so close. "Yes, it's me! I made a wish so I could speak to you, and it brought me here."

My father gasped and held his breath for a long pause. "Then... you are a true djinn?"

I pushed my magic toward them, creating a soft breeze in the darkness. For some reason, it was all I was capable of at the moment. "A very tired djinn by the feel of it."

"Fates, that's her signature, Alain. I would know that scent of jasmine anywhere. But there's so much more than I remember."

I reached through the bars into the darkness, toward the voices, wild desperation creeping into my mind. I had to hug them. "I'm here to help, but I can't sense your signatures. Are you in separate cells? Is there light?"

"We're wearing magicuffs. The guards put out the lights for the night," my mother said.

Across the darkness, iron clanged softly as someone pushed against the bars. A fingertip brushed against mine. Hard, calloused. My father? Fifteen years had passed since I'd last held his hand. A sob erupted from my throat at the fleeting touch. "I wish I could see you."

I can help with that. Is it safe?

Spark. I must have pulled him with me when I made the wish. Joy flooded my veins. He was *always* there.

It was wise he hadn't revealed himself yet, but we could probably risk it.

"I can make light. Will it draw the guards?" I asked my parents.

"No..." My father's voice was hesitant, clearly uncertain. "We should be safe with dim light. They've left us for the night, and there aren't many others in these cells right now."

Spark appeared, glowing dimly, and taking the form of a little dragon.

For one second, I saw the faces of my parents. Then, their joy dissolved into looks of absolute terror as pandemonium broke out in their cell.

"It's him, it's a trick! The Illumined One!" My father gasped and shoved my mother against the wall at the back of the cell, putting his body between us.

My mother started sobbing. "Why do you torment us? What else do we have to lose?"

Horror quaked through me as the fantasy I'd imagined since I was twelve devolved into a nightmare. My parents cowered in fear across from me as I shoved my hands through the bars. "It's me. Your daughter! I swear I'm really here. There's nothing to be afraid of!"

My father pointed to Spark. "That dragon, it's a monster!"

"What? This is Spark, my familiar. He's a fire sprite, not a dragon. Spark, turn into anything else!"

The dragon poofed into a tiny floating candle, and my parents froze, too terrified to move.

This wasn't how this was supposed to go. I pushed myself against the bars, overwhelmed by my pounding heartbeat. "Spark has watched over me since my first planes-walk. What are you afraid of?"

"The Illumined One. The lord of this place," my mother whispered.

"A massive, glowing crystal dragon. He's our master,

and his manifestations haunt these halls," my father added, not moving an inch.

"Where are we?" I asked.

"The Realm of Earth."

Well, shit.

The Realm of Earth was my opposite plane. According to my friend Amira, my magic would work like crap here, and I wouldn't be able to planes-walk away. Gods, I hoped I could at least fly.

"That explains why I feel like utter crap." I stopped struggling against the bars and slowly inhaled a rasping breath of air, stale, dank, and filled with dust. The walls vibrated with a sickly energy that weighed down on me, and my arms felt like lead. Yup, the Realm of Earth definitely hated me.

I was trapped. *We* were trapped.

I examined the hard and frightened features of my parents in the dim light. They were far older than I remembered them. Gray hair, weathered skin, and many scars.

My heart ached. "How long have you two been here?"

My parents exchanged looks before my mother spoke. "When you planes-walked away, we looked for you everywhere. After months of searching the realms, we ended up here. We knew that the Illumined One took prisoners to work in his mines and thought you might have been captured. Instead, his agents took us prisoner in the merchant's town. Has it really been a decade and a half since you left?"

My gods. I'd done this to them. Forced them into servitude in this dark hellhole while I'd gone about my life. I was the worst daughter ever.

Tears burned my eyes, and I nodded. "I'm so sorry."

"It's okay honey. It hasn't been all that bad. While we've been trapped here a long time, we've only been in this cell for a couple of days. The important thing is you're alive and we're together," my mom said, reaching toward me.

I flinched. "I'm gonna get us out of here. I promise."

"How?" my father asked, sorrow in his voice.

"Spark, can you cut through the bars?"

Hmm, he said. *Might be hard, but we can cut through the locks. Summon your blade.*

I summoned my khanjar, and my parents flinched. Clearly, their stay here had not been kind. I'd make that crystal dragon pay for what he'd done, but first we had to get out of these cells.

Spark disappeared, and his flames poured through my tattoos and into my blade. While the Realm of Earth was draining my magic, I could feel the full strength of his power in my veins, and relief flooded through me. Spark's fire magic mixed with Damian's magic in the dagger, and their familiar signatures surged around me.

This might be our ticket out.

The blade's glow changed from dull orange to white

hot. I reached through the bars and wedged the blade into the U-shaped shackle of the padlock. My wrists ached as I twisted the blade.

The iron sparked and sent up a noxious plume of smoke as the knife's magic began to slowly cut through the shackle. Then, with a metallic pop, the padlock broke free and clattered to the ground.

I lifted the latch, and the cell door creaked as I pushed my way into the hallway. I crossed to my parent's cell, and they grabbed me through the bars, pulling me close. My mother kissed my hands. "It's really you."

My chest ached, and I couldn't see through the water in my eyes. I pushed my face against the bars, grabbing at my father's shoulder with my free hand. I clung to them as if I could make up for fifteen years apart.

I never wanted to let go, but I had to get us out of this cursed place. Steeling myself, I wiped my eyes. "How much time until the guards check in?"

My mom glanced down the dark hall. "Probably a few hours, but we don't really know since we haven't been in here long. We tried to escape, and they put us in here."

My heartache erupted into rage, like oil catching fire. I rammed my white hot khanjar into the lock on their cell door and snapped it with a furious twist.

Dismissing the blade, I wrenched the door open, and my parents stumbled out into my arms.

My rage vanished instantly as I hugged them, not

daring to let go. I'd ached for this moment for fifteen years, and it was finally here. I'd finally gotten my deepest wish. If the guards showed up, I'd kill them. If the Illumined One himself came down, I'd shatter him into dust. This moment was mine, and I wouldn't let fear or demons, or anything take it from me.

7

Neve

After the tears ran out and our arms were too sore to hold each other any longer, my parents brought me up to speed on what we were up against.

It was pretty damn dire.

If I had to pick one thing worse than being trapped in the Realm of Earth, it would be being trapped in a labyrinth *in* the Realm of Earth—and that, of course, was where we were.

Did the fates have some special maze-vendetta against me?

We were trapped deep in the mines of the Illumined One, a vast complex of tunnels inhabited by his workers and minions.

As if that wasn't enough, the only way out was

through the crystal dragon's lair. Apparently, he was the size of a jumbo jet and entirely evil.

I turned to my parents. "I'd rather be covered in fire ants than have to find our way out through this maze. Can one of you try wishing us out of here?"

My father furrowed his brow. "I'm not sure that's how it works. I'm not a full djinn like you, but I remember some of the family lore. You made a wish to get here, and if you only recently transitioned, then it will take time to recover that power. Days, weeks—I don't know. I'm not sure it would work anyway since we're in the Realm of Earth."

My heart sank. My father, born a half-djinn like me, had some idea of how our ancestral powers worked. He'd never become a true genie, so I hoped he was wrong on the wishes front.

"Let's try anyway. Mom, wish us back to the Hall of Inquiry in Magic Side."

She squeezed my hand and spoke in a commanding voice, "I wish that you would transport all three of us safely back to the Hall of Inquiry in Magic Side, Chicago."

Nothing, not even a fizzle of power.

I had them try again, but it was pointless. My genie powers had gone to Majorca on vacation, and fates only knew when they would return.

"Spark, can you planes-walk out and warn Damian what's happened?"

Sorry, not possible. This place is shielded from teleportation and planes-walking. Your wish broke the rules, but I cannot leave on my own, he said.

Damn it.

"Who's Damian?" my mother asked.

Uh-oh.

I brushed it off. "A powerful friend. He may be able to help, but it doesn't matter, because it looks like we're on our own."

My parents nodded. Both looked determined, as if it would be as simple as walking out. As if they believed in me.

Guilt clawed at my heart, and I scrunched my fingers into my hair in exasperation. "This is all my fault. I screwed up the wish. I should have just pulled you to me... I meant to, but I just couldn't control my magic."

My father pressed his palm to my shoulder. A once familiar sensation, long forgotten. "The way I understand it, powers like yours take decades to learn, longer to master. If you can do what you've done after only a few days, then you're far ahead of the curve. I have no doubt that you can get us out of here, wish or no wish."

The blood drained from my face. There was no worse pressure than having the people you love believe in you when they shouldn't.

My mother rubbed my hand. "We'll get out together."

I fought down the fear, worry, and anger that bubbled up. "Okay, let's go."

My mother jingled the magicuffs around her wrists. "Any chance you—or your little friend—know how to get these off? I haven't tossed a spell in decades, and I'm so eager I can practically taste my own magic."

When I was a child, I'd assumed that my mother was a half-djinn like my dad and me. I was wrong. It explained where I got my knack for spells.

I'll help if I can be a dragon again, Spark said.

I glared at Spark who was still in the little bobbing candle. "That's not charitable."

Why should I hide who I am?

I scratched the back of my head, somewhat embarrassed. "Do you mind if Spark becomes a dragon again?"

My mom shrugged, which Spark took as an okay, morphing back into his dragon form. My parents jumped back and watched him with palpable unease, but they dealt with it.

"How do we do this?" I asked the sprite. "Last time we had Damian's magic and a big hammer. And it hurt a lot."

We'd also had Damian's healing magic. I glanced nervously at my haggard parents, not sure how much abuse they could take.

"We can handle a little pain," my mother said, without missing a beat. "You've no idea what we've been through in here. Personally, I would scrub myself with a rabid porcupine if I could cast a spell again."

My father pushed down a smile, but his eyes twinkled.

Spark hovered in front of us. *Let's try cutting through the cuffs, like we did the locks.*

I summoned my khanjar and pulled Spark's magic into me. His power made me feel normal again in the absence of my own magic.

My father wanted to go first, just in case there were major burns, but my mother muscled him out of the way. "Not a chance, Alain. I'm not spending one more minute in these than I have to."

She braced her cuff against the bars of the cage, and I cut through the hinge with my super-heated khanjar, using it like an arc welder. Magic and metal sparked as I used my weight to push through the cuff. My mother gritted her teeth in pain as the metal heated up, and I had to stop partway to cool it off with my feeble wind magic. My father held her and shut his eyes.

Finally, the cuff snapped and fell away. My mother shook her hand, letting out the pain at last. "Whoa, Nelly, that smarts. But it's good to be free. Now the other."

I glanced at the red blisters on her wrist, and guilt dug into my stomach.

My mom followed my gaze and smiled. "That's going

to leave a beautiful scar. I've got so many, but I think that will be my favorite."

She was relentlessly cheerful, like Rhiannon, but that didn't make the task any better.

I couldn't get the image of the burns out of my head and cutting through the second shackle while my mom attempted to hold back tears was the worst thing I'd ever had to do.

Finally, after two short breaks to cool off the metal, I burned through the last of the brass.

My mom gasped, and her signature surged around me. Scents of clover and the taste of licorice. The feel of soft sheets.

I fought back the tears that sprang to my eyes. It was like getting kicked in the chest. I'd forgotten my mother's signature. If asked, I might have said licorice, but nothing like this. I wrapped my arms around her and breathed in as much as my lungs could hold.

I ended up coughing on the dusty air and laughing.

This was the magic that had followed me around the house as a child. Watched over me at night, held me when I'd cried. My mother ran her blistered and scarred hands through my hair, muttering thanks.

Finally, she turned to my father, and magic sparked in her hands. Her pupils dilated. "Oh honey, it feels *good* to have my magic back."

He held out his wrists, his blue eyes raging like the sea. "What are we waiting for?"

My mother helped by casting freezing spells as I worked on cutting through my father's magicuffs. I knew so little about her and her powers, and my heart leapt at all there was to learn. There was so much I didn't know about them both.

Halfway through, the combination of my fire and my mother's ice shattered the metal. The second cuff came off just as quick, leaving only minor blisters on my father's wrists.

As soon as his second cuff split, my father's signature washed over me. It was faint. As a half-djinn, his power was repressed in the Realm of Earth just like mine, but I could still pick out all the once forgotten notes.

His magic was tart, like ripe lemons, and sounded like trees swaying in the wind. It smelled like crisp clean paper. This was the magic of the man who'd tucked me in at night and read me stories of far-off lands, deserts, and genies. A deep ache lodged in my throat as the memories came flooding back.

I finally understood why I felt so at home in the Archives. So much of what I'd become and what I'd been was wrapped up in these two signatures. And now they enveloped me in a warm cocoon of long-forgotten memories.

I grabbed my parents and hugged them to me, drawing strength and joy from their magic. I knew the moment couldn't last, but I drew it out, breath by breath, for as long as I could.

Finally, I broke away from their arms. "Okay, let's get practical. How do we get out of here?"

My father squeezed my hand one last time before letting go. "The Illumined One has shielded the mines from teleportation magic. That way, no one can teleport in, steal gems, and teleport out again. However, there are portals to the other realms in the Merchant Town outside the City of Light."

"Okay, what's the City of Light and how do we get there?"

"The City of Light is the Illumined One's lair—a massive cavern with a city built inside. It's also shielded from teleportation, but there is a gateway to the Merchant Town. We've never been beyond the City of Light, but I know there's a lot of traffic coming and going," my mother said.

"That's right." My father rubbed his hands together thoughtfully. "Our overlords turned the upper tunnels into cells like these as well as shanty towns, where we used to live. Currently, we're in the mines, but not too deep. We're close to the exit, so that's good news."

Fewer maze-like passages was *always* good news. "Right. Step one, we get the heck out of these mines."

Spark dimmed his glow, and we snuck to the entrance of the cell block. Unfortunately, the door was bolted shut. Spark turned into a bobbing light and slipped through the tiny window.

No sentries out here. There's another lock, but I think I can melt it.

I peeked through the tiny window. Spark shifted back to a dragon and blew a jet of flame on the padlock. The door slowly began to glow red until the fire cut through the lock. Spark slid the deadbolt back, and the door slowly creaked open.

My parents instinctively jumped back at the sight of the glowing dragon on the other side, still unsettled by his form.

Waiting a beat to be certain there was nobody ahead, I crept into the corridor and motioned for my parents to follow. Instead of lights and torches, the passage was illuminated by a fluorescent purple fungus that grew along the walls, giving everything an eerie pinkish glow.

I considered bringing a sample back to my friends at the Field Museum, but then thought better of it.

We wound our way through the claustrophobic tunnels. The air was stale and heavy with dust, and every breath was a struggle. I couldn't get out of there soon enough.

Left, right, left. Left. My brain hurt, but my parents knew the mine well...I hoped. I was certainly lost beyond all comprehension.

Thankfully, I didn't have to do this alone.

The sound of stone dragging against stone tore me from my reverie.

Two hulking terracotta warriors swung into the corridor in front of us. They had clay armor, demonic faces, and sharp spears. Before I could cry out a warning, my father whipped his hands up and a weak gust of wind shoved one of the warriors into the wall.

A thin crack spread along the warrior's right shoulder, then he flung his spear forward with surprising speed. The feathered shaft whistled in the air, and the tip grazed my father's face.

The other warrior hurled his spear at my mother. She yelped as it whizzed past her head. Thrusting both her hands out, she began reciting a spell. Crackling lightning leapt from her hands and cascaded across the body of the warrior. My mother gritted her teeth, and her signature surged. With a thunderclap, the sentry exploded into a cloud of dust.

My father toppled the other guard with a well-placed gust of wind. Its clay armor fractured as it crashed to the ground.

I was on it in a flash.

Kicking the spear from the sentry's hands, I summoned my khanjar and rammed it into one of the narrow cracks. Using my weight to lever the blade, the fracture widened, and then with a sudden release, the warrior's clay body split in two.

Everything was still.

I collapsed against the wall, completely out of breath in the suffocating realm.

"Oh, that felt good!" My mother beamed.

"Yes," my father said, dusting off his hands. "A lot of fun, but it also made a lot of noise. This place will be crawling with clay heads soon."

I nodded. "Then we'd better make a run for it."

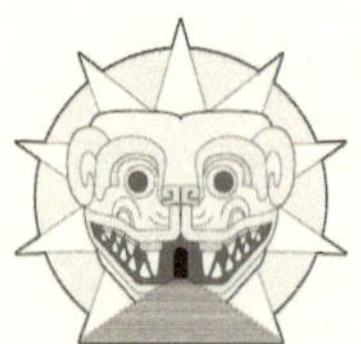

8

Damian

Lily's finger had landed on a point labeled the City of Light located in the Realm of Earth. None of us had ever heard of it.

Neither had anyone at the Order.

Every part of me wanted to planes-walk there immediately, but we would need some idea of what we were getting into, so Rhiannon and I called every researcher we knew and set them on the task.

Finally, one of the imps at the Archives texted Rhiannon back with a snippet.

She grimaced as she read. "Entrance to the City of Light is impossible. It's ruled by some sort of god-like being known as the Illumined One. There is, however, a town on the outskirts where merchants from the other planes meet and trade in the city's great wealth in gemstones and precious metals. There are portals there."

She looked up. "That's all."

"Great. Another mysterious forbidden city. Well, if we got into Helwan, we can get in here. Sounds like our access point is the merchant bazaar. You're coming, I assume?"

Rhiannon nodded. "If I could planes-walk, I would have left you here already."

I liked her fire. "I can use the Atlas of the Planes to get us there. Ready?"

She nodded.

I looked back to Lily. "Thank you, for everything. My people will reach out to you shortly to settle up."

Lily smiled. "Good luck, you two."

I grabbed Rhiannon's arm and placed my other hand on the book, focusing my mind on the City of Light. While the map of the Realm of Air had shown hundreds of floating islands, the map of the Realm of Earth showed a web of cities connected by winding passages.

The Atlas tugged at me, pulling me forward, and the taste of dust filled my mouth as the City of Light zoomed into view.

The city was blocked by a teleportation barrier. Drawing my mind deeper, I focused instead on the little village beside the City of Light—Merchant Town.

A storm of sand whirled up around us. The sudden vortex of magic tore at every fiber of our being, threatening to rip Rhiannon out of my grasp. I tightened my grip as we rocketed through the cosmos, spinning and whirling until we slammed down in the middle of a crowded square.

Rhiannon staggered forward, and I caught her. She was pale and unsteady.

"Holy shit." She wheezed. "How do you guys not hurl every time you do that?"

I shut my eyes and ignored her, focusing on Neve.

My dragon sense roared, and fire filled my veins. Our connection was back, an anchor cable screaming and shaking under the strain of the sea. It was so strong I jerked forward. "She's here. Far away, but here."

Rhiannon clenched her fist. "Hell yes! But where are we?"

The square we were in was crowded with merchant stalls and marketgoers. We caught a few odd glances, but most had ignored our arrival. Neve and I had received a similar reception in the Realm of Air.

Our modern clothing would be a problem. From the discordant display of styles, I assumed there were many travelers, but we would still stick out.

Rhiannon looked up. "I think we're in a cavern, but I can't see the ceiling. Fates, this place is huge."

I understood the map a little better now. "I suspect most of the realm is solid rock. The cities occupy caverns connected by tunnels."

"One giant, freaking ant colony," Rhiannon whispered.

Perhaps.

I started pushing forward in the direction of Neve. "Let's go."

People cleared a path around us as I let my aura flare. As a FireSoul and fallen angel, with a mix of stolen efreeti powers and ice magic, my signature was probably overwhelming. Nature's way of saying *do not touch*.

Three elaborately carved stone gateways flanked the square—open portals to the Realms of Air, Water, and Fire, glowing white, blue, and red, respectively. At least that gave us an exit if we couldn't planes-walk out of the City of Light.

"You know where we're headed?" Rhiannon asked, close at my side.

"No, but my magic is pulling me straight toward her."

I pointed to a massive gateway in the distance flanked by two fearsome dragon statues. Sentries checked people as they passed through. "Unfortunately, we have to find a way through that."

Neve

Light.

My heart thundered with hope.

Could this be the end of the mines at last?

It had taken us two hours to get through. The distance hadn't been far, but we'd picked our way slowly and taken time to avoid as many sentries as possible. Despite my parents' deep-seated desire for vengeance, we didn't want to raise any alarms by leaving a trail of destruction in our wake.

Spark had been able to scare off most of the mine's human denizens by taking the form of a glowing crystal dragon. It had pretty much the same effect on them as his original appearance had on my parents. Sheer terror.

And now, we were almost out.

Thank fates my parents knew where they were going. I would have been five miles in the other direction or tricked by an evil demon sprite by now if I were on my own.

The brightness at the end of the tunnel was almost overwhelming, like driving into the sun. I shielded my eyes, barely able to make out the forms standing along the walls.

Dread bore down on me. More terracotta warriors, maybe ten along each side.

I returned to my parents, who were crouched down about twenty feet back, just around the curve. "Good news—I think we've found the end of the tunnel. Bad news? The exit is blocked by about twenty clay heads."

My mother's eyes twinkled. "That's all very good news. Sentries mean we're at the exit. The City of Light is just beyond. Hopefully, once we get past the clay warriors, we can slip unseen into an alley."

"Getting past being the key," my father muttered.

My mother rubbed her hands together. "I'm more than happy to start blasting them."

My father shook his head. "Too many, love. Even with the element of surprise, we'd be instantly overrun. We need to lure them away or at least reduce their numbers."

"Spark, can you make a distraction? Lure them off?"

Yup, he said.

I nodded. My parents couldn't hear him, of course. Nobody could, in fact, except Damian.

My chest tightened at the thought of him. I didn't understand why he could hear my familiar.

My mother pursed her lips and tapped on the wall. "If your dragon can lead them down the passage past us, I can conceal us in darkness. We can hide in one of the side tunnels back there."

Time was ticking. This was our best chance. "Let's do it."

Spark turned into a little bobbing light and drifted ahead while we scuttled down the hall and veered right into an empty side passage.

My mother moved her hands, and the licorice and clove scent of her magic filled the air. She spun shadows like cloth and pulled them around us, cloaking us in darkness. My heart clenched with memories. Was this how she put me to sleep at night? I barely remembered that.

We waited in darkness, holding our breath.

Suddenly, a crash of shattering clay echoed through the hall. Moments later, a translucent flaming dwarf ran by waving its arms like a lunatic.

Spark.

That was one weird distraction.

His voice rang in my mind. *Knocked them down like dominoes. Left a couple for you. I'll catch up.*

I smiled as Spark did a backflip and ran off as half a dozen statues charged down the hall after him.

As soon as they passed, I summoned my khanjar, and we darted out of the shadows.

Green magic crackled around my mother's hands. "Showtime."

We whipped around the bend, and I slammed straight into one of the guards. Shoving it back with a burst of wind, I rammed my khanjar into its chest. Damian's signature tugged at my senses as the magic blade sliced into the terracotta, and the sentry's torso shattered.

Even if Damian wasn't here right now, the feel of his magic in my khanjar calmed me. Had he known it would have this effect on me when he forged it?

A large crash—the sound of pottery breaking—sounded on my right as my mother blasted another guard. I ducked as he exploded outward in a cloud of dust and crackling green magic. Stone shrapnel ripped across my skin, and I grimaced.

Before I could recover, a spear whistled through the air straight at me. A sudden blast of air knocked it away, and I nodded thanks to my father.

The clay warrior ahead of me drew a curved blade from his sheath, and I charged. Using a burst of air to boost my momentum, I slammed my shoulder into his chest. Pain ricocheted through my bones as the warrior reeled backward and shattered against the ground.

My mother dispatched the last warrior with bolts of crackling blue lightning. Man, she was loaded.

I sucked in a breath of stale air and gagged. "That's all, I think."

A pile of broken statues lined the far wall like fallen dominoes, just as Spark had said. He got four or five for sure. *Clever sprite.*

My father sucked his teeth. "I'm afraid I'm not much help in a fight."

I grabbed his hand. "I would have been a shish kabab without you. We'd better go before the rest come back."

We stumbled out of the mouth of the tunnel into the blinding light. It took my eyes a second to focus.

The gateway to the mines was carved like a dragon's mouth with pillars like bared teeth. We rushed out of the jaws onto a monumental stairway. Below us, a small city of two- and three-story buildings filled an impossibly large cavern. At its center, there was a light so blinding that I had to look away almost instantly.

Black shadows swam in front of my eyes.

"Quickly now. We need to get into the cover of the houses. *He* can see all that is illuminated with his light." My father took my arm, and we scrambled down the stairs, across an open square, and into the winding back alleys of the city. Thankfully, the square around the entryway was deserted.

We turned left and right until I was completely lost, and hopefully, any potential pursuers were lost as well. We wound our way through a dark alley. The light at the center of the city was like a spotlight, with little diffusion. Everything was either bathed in brilliant light or left in deep shadow.

"What is that light? It's so bright," I hissed.

"The Illumined One," my father whispered. "His body is made of pure crystal, and his heart glows like the sun. He sleeps atop a hoard of gems and precious things piled in the center of the city, hence its name, the City of Light."

I craned my neck upward and a moment of vertigo twisted through my body. The sides of the cavern were a vivid green. Plants of all types draped down from caves and recesses in the rock, and the scents of flowers and fruit trees overwhelmed my senses. "And all these plants grow because of his light?"

"They are the best source of fresh produce in this

realm. He guards his orchards jealously, and his agents trade the harvest at exorbitant prices."

My mouth watered at the scent of oranges. Their aroma was intoxicating, and my mother followed my gaze and rested a hand on my arm. "Thieves get their hands cut off and their tongues pulled out."

My stomach churned. What a horrid place to live, surrounded by piles of treasure you could never own and the perfume of fruits you could never taste.

We maneuvered through the back alleys of the city, staying out of sight, keeping to the dark shadows. My mother used her magic to extend them, cloaking us in darkness as we moved. Everything around us was cold, lifeless stone. We saw few people and spoke to no one.

I pointed to a peddler in white robes, someone we could ask for directions, but my father shook his head and drew us into the shadow of a house. "The people here live their lives in the light of the Illumined One. His gaze is everywhere, like the rays of the sun. To disobey him is to die. Helping us would be a death sentence."

A shudder ran down my spine.

When the peddler passed by, we moved on.

"How do you know where to go?" I asked.

"Long ago, before our first escape attempt, we were permitted in this area," my mother explained, as we snuck along the back of a tall stone building. "There's a gateway to Merchant Town at the other side of the chamber. We're not far. Our mine was the closest of six. Good luck, really."

As we snuck through the city, I gave my parents a brief, whispered rundown of my life. Orphan, scholar, detective, full djinn. I omitted the whole working with a FireSoul and being chased by a genie-hoarding demon bit. Things were complicated enough without having to worry about that. Yet.

Spark finally caught up with us. He'd assumed the form of a bobbing light and was practically invisible in the surrounding glare. He stayed high, scanning for signs of pursuit.

It became harder to avoid people as foot traffic increased. We would stick out like three racoons in a chicken coop. I was decked out in jeans and a jacket, while my parents looked like, well, dirty runaway miners.

I scanned the rooftops. They were flat and barren, though a few had lines with white laundry drying in the light. "Spark, can you find us some clothes?"

On it. He zipped away through the sky.

I touched my father's shoulder gently. "You're half-djinn. Can you fly?"

"I used to. Not sure about here."

"We should try. We might need it."

"I can't," my mom snapped.

"She's a bit bitter about that. But she's got more magic than I'd know what to do with." A slight breeze rose around me, and my father floated quietly into the air a few feet off the ground. "Looks like I've still got it... but not much. This place is sucking me dry."

I tried joining him in the air. Floating was possible, but even harder than when I was first learning—no power whatsoever.

The joy of the moment extinguished any frustration I had. I was flying with my father. I could barely register it.

A long robe swept down the alley, and I nearly jumped out of my skin.

Spark. With laundry. It took him a few trips, but we were soon draped in ill-fitting white robes and head dresses.

It is hard to understand your proper size. Clothing makes no sense.

Wasn't *that* the truth.

"City folk cover themselves head-to-toe. The light of the Illumined One is said to burn exposed flesh," my mother explained.

At least it gave us plenty of cover.

We still kept to the alleys. The robes didn't hide our feet, and my boots screamed *intruder*, but at least we couldn't be identified from a distance.

Unfortunately, the streets got even busier. We kept our heads down, and at last, we reached the edge of a large market square. A massive gateway stood at the far end, flanked by two towering stone statues. They were like the clay warriors we'd fought earlier, just a hundred-or-so feet tall.

The way out.

I glanced back at the opposite end of the square into the blazing light of the Illumined One. It was too bright to make out the crystal dragon slumbering on its pile of gems and treasure. My head ached when I looked away, and spots swam before my eyes.

Time to get the hell out of here.

9

———

Neve

We strode out into the square, making our way toward the gateway. It had two towering stone doors that were open.

Thank fates.

I'd take all the small miracles I could get, because I was betting we'd have to get past an army of clay heads.

My mother adjusted her billowing robe. She was short and scrappy, and the hem dragged along behind her. "Hopefully, we can talk our way through. Your father and I know the local language. Don't say a word."

I nodded, and then suddenly jerked back on my heels.

A man dressed in all white yanked a fistful of my robe. He said something in a language I didn't understand and tugged again.

I smacked his hand away and cursed, immediately regretting it.

His eyes widened, and he snatched the front of my robe, glaring at my boots and shouting something. What, I had no idea, but it sounded bad, and my father's face went as white as his robe.

Damned boots.

At least they were good for something. I rammed my foot upwards into my assailant's balls. The man gasped and doubled over, so I took the opportunity to ram his face into my knee. "I think the jig is up! We've gotta run now!"

I took off through the market square, my parents close behind, as furious cries rose around us.

"Sorry!" I shouted.

"Served him right!" my mother yelled as she shoved a hapless bystander out of her way. "You don't even know what he said!"

Now I was curious, but there was no time. The gate loomed ahead. We were almost there.

The cavern shook as a deafening roar thundered through the air. It was as shrill as broken glass and as deep as an earthquake. My parents stumbled to their knees as small stones rained down around us.

My father's lips moved, but all I could hear was a high-pitched ring.

Pandemonium erupted as terrified marketgoers ran

for cover. I couldn't hear their screams. I shook my head, trying to clear the ringing in my ears.

What the hell was that noise?

My gut knew. The Illumined One had just woken.

I hauled my mom off the ground as my father staggered to his feet. He waved to us and started shouting. I couldn't make out the sounds, but I could read his lips well enough. *Get your mother! Run!*

I grabbed my mom by her elbow, and we hurried toward the gate. The massive stone doors began swinging shut.

"Spark! Can you do something about those doors?"

The dragon darted into the air. *Knock, knock.*

Spark shot forward, transforming into a blazing meteor mid-flight. He slammed into the right door, and it exploded in a cloud of dust and rubble.

Panic shot through me. "Spark! Are you okay?"

Slightly dizzy. Just a minute, he said.

Momentary relief flooded through me. His voice was distant, but he was okay, and we had a way out.

We skidded to a halt as the ground shuddered and ripped open in front of us, revealing a gaping chasm of jagged rock. My mother slipped, but my father caught her arm, and we pulled her back from the precipice.

The ground shook as the chasm widened. Horror clenched my gut as stone houses split in half and crumbled in a cascade of rubble.

This was all to stop us?

My stomach knotted. Everywhere I went, I brought chaos and destruction.

But I couldn't face that now. We were only a few hundred feet from the gate and had to focus on getting out. The chasm kept widening, though, quake by quake.

"Shit! Do you think we can fly?" I turned to my father, not sure if he could hear me.

He rose unsteadily into the air. "Barely. Perhaps between the two of us, we can carry your mother across."

His voice was like a faint echo in my ringing ears.

I nodded. We each grabbed an arm and rose into the air, slowly hovering across the growing trench, slowly losing altitude.

Please fates, have our backs.

Halfway across, we'd already dropped below the lip of the chasm. I had so little strength here.

Rage coursed through me, drowning my panic. This was not how I would lose my parents. I gritted my teeth and called the wind. A slight boost pushed us up.

But it was not enough.

We slammed into the far wall of the chasm, just at neck level. My father grabbed on with his free arm, and my mom grabbed hold with both hands. Summoning my khanjar, I slammed it into the ground and levered myself up over the ledge, panting. Turning, I dropped onto my stomach and grabbed my mother's wrists and heaved, pulling her kicking and scrabbling out of the abyss. My father, no longer having to hold her up, rose beside her.

The earth shook again, and I nearly tipped back into the rift. We scrambled from the edge as the lip began to crumble behind us.

A voice like a thousand shattering glasses ripped through the air. "They are stealing what is mine! Stop them."

The earth rumbled and shadows shifted around us. Terror shot through me. The Illumined One was moving.

With a cacophonous boom, the massive stone statues flanking the gate tore their feet off their pedestals and turned their vacant gazes on us.

Oh crap.

The hundred-foot-tall statues moved unnaturally fast. I shoved my parents out of the way as a stone spear buried itself deep in the earth where we'd been standing.

My mother wrenched free of my grip and stood, hands out, facing the colossal warriors. Green magic crackled around her, forming in her hands.

The second warrior hurled his spear straight at my mom. I snapped my hands up at the same time as my father, and we blasted it just out of the way with our feeble gusts of wind. The spear skidded across the ground and tipped into the chasm.

Magic cracked as my mother finished her spell. She

slung the green ball of magic at the slow-moving colossus. The spell burst into his leg, and emerald lightning crackled across his body.

His knee began to glow a pale green and then exploded outward in a burst of dust and rubble. The statue shuddered, and then began to topple forward, arms spreading wide.

My mother cackled with glee. "The bigger they are, the harder they fall!"

Who was this madwoman?

In retrospect, this probably explained a lot about my temperament.

I shot across the space between us and shoved her out of the way. We landed in the rocks and rubble as the stone warrior crashed to the ground behind us. It shattered into a cloud of dust and rock, and shrapnel tore across our backs.

"The smaller you are, the easier you squish," I muttered. Gritting my teeth against the pain in my shoulder blade, I pulled my mom to her feet. "You almost got pancaked."

"Just admiring my work... but maybe we should run. I need to recharge."

The earth shook as the second colossus stepped over the remains of his shattered companion and drew his spear from the ground.

"Good plan, Mom."

His mouth opened in an eerily silent howl of rage.

We bolted right, but he slammed his spear down in front of us, blocking our path, ready to sweep us off into the chasm.

My head snapped up as a black shape rose in the air behind him.

A beautiful angel with burning arms.

Damian. But how?

The dark angel landed on the head of the colossus and slammed his iron spear into its stone skull.

Thunder cracked, and I felt Damian's signature wash over me, sending heat straight through me and bringing tears to my eyes.

The statue opened its mouth in a silent roar as Damian's dark magic blasted out from its vacant eyes. It took a single step and then its face exploded, raining rubble down on top of us.

A jagged crack ripped down through the stone colossus like a zipper opening up. Damian leapt into the air as my mother and I darted between the legs of the faceless giant, beelining for the open gateway.

The statue slammed into the ground, shattering across the remains of the other sentinel. The earth quaked, sending us to our knees.

Damian was at my side in a second, pulling me up. "No time. Run!"

Before I could respond, the Illumined One's unearthly roar shook the cavern to its core.

My ears screamed, unable to take any more. My

father was at my side, shouting, but I couldn't make out his words.

Damian shoved us all past the broken doorway into a dark tunnel. Light and heat surged behind us. I looked back as a blinding ray of light reduced the remaining door into a waterfall of molten stone.

"Holy fates!" I screamed.

Rather than breathing out flames, the Illumined One released a beam of searing light.

Spark, in dragon form, soared overhead. *I wish I could do that. Maybe I will be big like him one day.*

Rhiannon appeared at my side, helping pull my father along the corridor.

"Rhia? You're here, too!"

"And not barbequed, miraculously!" I could barely hear her words. "I hope he can't stick his head into this hole, or we're gonna be fried chicken."

We staggered forward through the tunnel. The passage shook, and I lost my footing as bits of the ceiling collapsed around us. I crawled to my feet and barely made out a few travelers in the dim light ahead. They were screaming and stampeding toward the other end where dull light filtered in.

The way out.

The earth began to quake, not a single burst, but wave after wave. Stone poured from above in sheets and boulders.

"He's caving the tunnel in!" Rhiannon screamed.

Damian unleashed an enormous burst of cold, and a wall of ice formed across the ceiling above us. I assumed he was trying to support the rock, but the quake shattered it too, and ice shards rained down.

Then everything slowed. Rubble drifted downward like gentle snowflakes as Rhiannon's magic washed over us. She'd slowed time around us, but it would only last a few seconds.

"Run." She appeared to be screaming, but the words barely registered in my deafened and ringing ears.

We sprinted toward the light as time snapped back to normal behind us. A tsunami of stone and dust chased us down the passage.

We stumbled into the open square of what I assumed was the Merchant Town as the gateway to the City of Light collapsed inward behind us. I spun around, and my shoulders sagged with relief. We'd made it. All of us.

I sensed we were past the teleportation barrier that had enclosed the mines and the City of Light. But we were still in the Realm of Earth, and my powers were weakened. I grabbed Damian's arm. "I don't know if I can planes-walk us out."

Damian pulled me close and shouted over my shoulder. "Spark, we need to get out of here! Let's planes-walk everyone to the Realm of Fire, now!"

Before I could open my mouth, Spark and Damian's magic swirled around us in a maelstrom of flame.

Damian held me tightly, and we exploded through the cosmos.

Mind-rending seconds later, I collapsed onto a hardened flow of lava and sucked in a deep breath of air. It tasted acrid and stunk of brimstone, but it was the most wonderful breath I had ever taken.

Clambering off my knees, I wiped my bloodied palms on what was left of my shirt. My magic coursed through me like a breached dam. Gods it felt good.

I looked around.

Damian, Rhiannon, my mother and father, and Spark.

My family was here. All of them. For the first time in my life.

My body shook with terror and joy and fatigue, and tears streamed down my face as I wrapped my arms around my parents.

Eventually, I released my hold on my mother and wiped my eyes. Even with my magic restored to full strength, exhaustion tugged at me.

Stepping back, I bumped into Damian. I spun, suddenly just inches from his body. His signature tickled my senses, and heat—his or mine, I couldn't be sure—swept over me.

Joy pierced my heart, bringing me back to the moment I'd seen his shadow rise behind the colossus. The moment I'd known for sure everything would be all right. "You came for me."

Something flashed across his face, and then his expression hardened. "You saved yourself."

His signature left me spinning and drew me in like the ether. The world around us was barren and reeked of brimstone, but all I could see were his forest-green eyes, and all I could smell were ancient trees and sandalwood.

I took a sharp breath as he pulled me close. Without meaning to, I traced the strong lines of his jaw with my fingertips, as if my hand had a mind of its own. As if my body knew what I wanted. My gaze drifted to his lips, and I parted my mouth.

"Nevaeh, who is this?"

My father's question shattered the moment. My heart stopped, and my stomach dropped about ten feet. I burst from Damian's arms, my face as red and hot as the lava lake.

Oh. Gods.

My life had suddenly become *a lot* more complicated.

10

Neve

Introductions I didn't want to ever have to make: *Hey mom and dad. I know we've just reunited, but here's my guy friend. He's not really my boyfriend, but he went down on me once. There's probably something between us. Also, he's a crime lord, a fallen angel, and a FireSoul, and he may want to kill me to steal my powers. But he has a nice car.*

Rhiannon took one look at my wide-eyed panic and jumped to the rescue. "Mr. Malek is an independent contractor and a specialist on missing items. He recently helped Neve rescue me from the Realm of Air and helped save Magic Side from a terrible curse."

"Oh?" my mother said, looking from Damian to me. I made introductions all around and quietly thanked the fates for Rhiannon, the queen of positive spin.

I probably would have stuttered something horrific.

Like, *Oh him? This is the guy who released the djinn and who used to be pals with the asshole who is currently trying to bind me to his service.*

So good save, all and all.

But damn. Three hours into having my parents back, I was already looking for ways to lie to them.

My father politely reached his hand out to Damian, pretending not to notice my sudden and horrific embarrassment. "Thank you, Mr. Malek, for helping us get out. I don't think we could repay you."

My mother hugged Rhiannon. "And you, too, of course. Things were getting a bit dicey for us. Did you really stop time? It was extraordinary."

I'd introduced Rhia first, and I could already tell that my mom would treat her like a second daughter.

I closed my eyes. Separate worlds. I needed everyone in their separate worlds. Everything was too new. I didn't know what my parents were really like. Hell, I didn't even know what Damian was really like.

Rhiannon, though, she was my rock. I grabbed her hand, giving it a squeeze of thanks.

My mother wrinkled her nose as she surveyed the scorched and baren landscape. "Are we in hell?"

I shrugged. "The Realm of Fire. So essentially, yes."

Spark waddled over and narrowed his eyes. *The Realm is very beautiful. You could lounge on the white sand beaches that surround the ever-burning kerosene seas. Or take a hot mud bath in the steaming caldera lakes where the Fire-Birds hatch their young.*

I choked on a laugh. "Spark makes it sound like toxic Cancun, but I don't know."

The little dragon glared at me.

My mother frowned. "Why here? It's so... uh... unpopulated."

"It's not ideal, but it was the safest place I could think of in the moment," Damian explained. "If we ran for one of the three portals in Merchant Town, our pursuers could have followed us through. And Magic Side isn't safe right now for Neve. I knew Spark and I could use our magic to transport us to the Realm of Fire."

My father was about to ask something, but my mom quieted him with a wave and interjected. "Why isn't Magic Side safe for Neve? She told us she was a detective. She's not being pursued by criminals, is she?"

Her voice was tight, and I couldn't help but glance at Damian.

Oh fates. Separate circles. Separate circles.

I needed to explain the bigger picture, but I hadn't wanted to go over everything in the mines. There had been no time, and I didn't want to worry my parents. We had enough on our plate.

But where to start?

I dragged my hand through my hair. Summary was best. "Essentially, I'm being hunted by a half-demon mage who is collecting genies. He's created some sort of plane of chaos and is preparing to invade Magic Side. We have to stop him. He almost trapped me this morning."

My mother's eyes bugged out. "And here I thought we were deep in the mud."

The hot wind sprayed a dusting of sand across the hardened lava, and I took a slow breath. It was time to ask the big question.

I turned to my father, pushing hope down in my chest. "I have no idea how to control my genie magic, and I know nothing about my gifts. I'm terrified the mage is going to bind me before I can figure things out. You're part-djinn, too... can you help?"

My father smiled with saddened eyes. "When you were a child, I dreamt of teaching you to fly one day and how to channel the wind. But I suspect you have far surpassed my skill already. As to granting wishes, only a true djinn can teach you that. It's been generations since one emerged from our line, and the secrets of that magic are well guarded. I hate to say it, but we should probably visit your great-great-great grandmother, Mavia. She's a djinn queen and has centuries of knowledge."

I never knew I had a grandparent. Elation replaced the sinking sense of failure in my heart. "I'm related to a queen? Holy fates."

My mother screwed up her face like a skunk had just gone nuclear. "Unfortunately, yes."

My father turned to her and narrowed his eyes. "Mavia's our best chance for helping Neve, dear."

"Oh, to be sure, but maybe I'll just head back to the mines while you visit."

He shrugged apologetically. "Queen Mavia can be—"

"A horrid bitch?" my mother suggested.

My father winced. "Yes, she can be difficult."

I shook my head. "Difficult doesn't matter. I can handle difficult. Until I understand my powers, we're all in peril. Queen Mavia sounds like my best shot. How do I find her?"

My father tugged at his beard. "She lives in an ice palace—"

"Which is fitting," my mother interjected.

He glared but continued. "A *magnificent* palace in the upper reaches of the Realm of Air. I can take you there, but perhaps not everyone."

"This could help." Damian waved his hand in the air, and a shimmering book materialized from the ether. The *Atlas of the Planes.*

He opened it to the Realm of Air and laid it down on the black rock. "Alain, can you pick out her location? Between you, Neve, and myself, we should be able to transport all of us. I don't like the idea of splitting up."

My father eyed him suspiciously. "You're a man of many talents, Mr. Malek. A fallen angel and a planes-walker? That is unusual."

Damian shrugged, and my stomach knotted.

Before the *loaded question train* pulled to a complete stop at the station, I hurried over to the Atlas and looked *real* interested. "Where's Mavia's palace?"

My father nodded, crouched down, and tapped his finger on the map. "Here. On the Island of Argyre."

I bit my lip and nodded. "Then that's where we're headed."

11

Damian

We stumbled from the ether and biting cold cut my skin.

We arrived in the middle of a teleportation platform perched on a jagged promontory at the far end of a floating island.

Neve shivered. I placed my palm at the base of her back and pushed a little warmth into her with my fire magic. She could draw on it herself, but she was transfixed with the view.

She shivered and turned to me, her cheeks flushed. Desire and need flashed through her eyes, and I fought the urge to wrap her in my arms.

The palace of Queen Mavia towered above the glassy mist. It was a tall, twisting spire perched precariously on an icy crag. The patchwork light gave its austere form an opalescent glow.

A rainbow of light filtered through the icy mist that covered the ground. It reminded me of the cloud towers of the angels. Not that I would ever venture into those realms again.

Facing that tower, Neve shone like a queen. Her red hair whipped in the bitter wind, the most brilliant color in the cold and drab expanse. She was like the sun breaking through the clouds.

Rhiannon sucked in a deep breath and coughed on the frigid air. She grabbed Neve's arm to steady herself. "I think—no—*I know* that I truly hate planes-walking."

"Feeling a little rough?" I asked. Her face was ashen. Planes-walking took some getting used to.

She groaned. "That's three times today. Earth. Fire. Air. We can collect the whole set in one trip if we head to water next. Maybe nobody will notice me vomit there."

"Please don't do it here," Neve teased. "It would freeze straight to the ground."

Rhia covered her mouth. "Gods, Neve. I may never be able to eat a Chicago dog again."

Tinaya sidled up to her daughter. "Isn't it delightful here? What more could you ask for? If I had unlimited resources and was going to create an enormous palace, I would make one just like this. Who needs things like beaches, warm water, and living plants or animals, when you can have so many different types of ice and snow?"

A winding path of steps descended from the teleportation platform down to the palace. Everything was sheathed in ice, but that was easily taken care of.

Neve jumped as I summoned the efreet's magic and bathed the icy steps in flame. Water melted away, instantly freezing again in rivulets as it ran down the sides of the stairs.

Tinaya leaned close to Neve and whispered, "He'd make a good groundskeeper. Strange, though, for an angel to have fire magic."

Neve's face tightened.

She expertly dodged the question. "I can channel fire magic, too. From my familiar."

Her tattoos illuminated with red light as she summoned Spark's magic though their bond. She quickly joined me at the steps, melting a path with blasts of fire.

She leaned close and muttered, "My folks are curious about you."

Quite.

I moved down a few stairs to give her space. "Perhaps trying to kiss me wasn't wise."

She gave me a demur smile from above. "Perhaps. But it would have been nice."

I couldn't help but gaze at her lips, flushed with the warmth of her fire.

Yes, it would have been nice.

Those lips would have stolen my breath, warm and wet, and pressed against mine. Her tongue would have grazed mine, and there would have been nothing left in the world.

Heat flashed through me, but in that moment, surrounded by her family, I knew that I was an intruder in their story. A thing that children were taught to fear. A monster.

I could tell by the light in Neve's eyes that something broken had been made whole. Her parents had given her something that I could never give her. Something threatened by my very presence. I wouldn't destroy that for her.

I was playing with fire, and it was time to stop.

Her gaze sought mine, and I shook my head. "It's best if I leave. The marid king knew instantly what I was and banished me from his realm. Queen Mavia might do the same. My presence may cause problems."

Not only that, but I had to find Matthias so I could ram my blade through his heart. Only then would Neve be safe from us both.

"Don't leave. If I have to face a djinn queen, I want you there at my side." She tried joining me on the step, but I shifted further down the melted path.

"That's probably the last place I should be."

Suddenly, I could barely stand to be this close to her. Her signature raged around me, a deadly siren's song. Except I wasn't the one being lured to my death.

I poured my frustration into the fire.

Why had fate cursed me with this relentless desire? The dragon within me was like a rabid beast, writhing and screaming to be let free.

No. I wouldn't allow it.

Neve pushed the mist away as we approached Mavia's palace. The landscape was pure ice. It coated the walls and towers. Light reflections danced across the frozen world, and the whole tower seemed to glow.

While the light of the Illumined One had been flat and lifeless, the light here was playful and full of color.

As we approached the massive entryway, a loud crack split the air, and the doors of the palace shook. Their coating of ice broke away and crumbled to the ground, as one of the doors swung inward.

The hairs on my neck stood on end. "Apparently, our arrival has been noticed."

Tinaya kicked one of the chunks that had been covering the door. The broken edge revealed dozens of thin layers, built up over time, like banded sandstone.

"The ice over the door is pretty thick. Doesn't seem anyone has come by in a long time." She glanced at Alain, a smile on her lips. "I wonder why?"

Her father fixed her with a flat stare, but his eyes were laughing. "Please, remember civility, dear. I don't want us to end up in another prison. I've heard all your jokes a thousand times."

Neve looked away, hiding tears in her eyes. I could almost feel her emotion in her magic. Joy and sorrow.

My heart twisted. She had missed so much.

What would her life have been like with parents like these—parents who could still laugh and have light in their eyes after fifteen years of servitude and torment?

Neve bit her lip, focusing on the ground.

To lose her freedom was one thing, but to have these people ripped from her life... I wouldn't let that happen. If I had to sell my soul to the heavens or hells, I wouldn't let Matthias have her.

Neve slipped through the door, her father following right behind.

This could be a trap. I raced forward into the darkness, my eyes taking a second to adjust after the blinding white of the ice. I stopped cold in my tracks.

Two enormous ice devils blocked our path, frozen spikes protruding from their craggy limbs. One stepped toward Neve.

I whipped my black sword from the ether, and fire erupted from the blade. The memory of the attack on the *Jewel of Tayir* fueled my rage.

"Wait!" Alain's voice cracked through the air with an

unexpected tone of command. "These are the queen's servants."

He turned to the devils. "We're here to see Queen Mavia. We seek urgent assistance. Let us pass."

The ice devils drew their cavernous eyes toward Neve, and her hands flickered with Spark's fire magic.

The ice devil's voice rumbled like an avalanche. "Fire is forbidden outside of the queen's hearths."

My palms itched. Something made me want to cut them down, but these weren't the same monsters that had attacked Neve when we were aboard the *Jewel*. Probably.

Gritting my teeth, I dismissed my blade. Neve followed, releasing the fire from her hands.

The devils loomed over Alain. "Your identity is known. If you will vouch for your companions, proceed."

He stared up, unafraid. "I do. Let us pass."

A pair of human attendants in fur-lined robes swept into the room and led us on. What kind of people chose to serve in a place like this?

We left the cold and silent entranceway and entered a great hall. Six great hearths blazed with magical fires that consumed no wood.

Sunlight streamed in through the high stained-glass windows, creating lively patterns of light along the stone walls. In comparison to the monochrome ice world outside, the hall was a vibrant picture in light.

Perhaps the palace was only frozen on the outside.

The attendants swung open the doors to a colonnaded throne room. And there, upon a dais of frozen shards, sat Queen Mavia.

Fearsome, statuesque, and indomitable.

With a glare as cold as ice.

12

Neve

The warmth of the great hall vanished as the throne room doors swung open.

My breath caught. Queen Mavia.

The air in the room seethed with power, and the queen's signature slammed into me like an avalanche. My mind whirled, disoriented and lost.

Her magic was frigid. Not like the ice around us, but cold like iron in the depth of winter. So cold your flesh would freeze to it instantly, and you'd have to rip your skin to free your hand. It sounded like the howling winter wind and tasted like fresh snow. Yet there was a warm hint of allspice, and something about it felt almost... indescribable. Like the strength of snowdrops pushing up in spring. She was resplendent. Her face, perfection. Posture immaculate.

The ice around her throne was ever changing. Melting from her warmth and refreezing in crystalline forms. This woman terrified me in ways the djinn never had. Her power felt inevitable and absolute.

Could she be my ally in all this?

"Enter." Her voice cut through the air like shattering icicles.

I stepped into the throne room and noticed we weren't alone.

Ice devils lurked in the corners of the room, clinging to the walls like spiders. Four attendants held a pair of massive, hairy mastiffs at bay. Incongruously, a small dog sat on the Queen's lap, tongue out and eyes delighting in the world around it. She scratched its head and shot me a quick glare that made me snap to attention.

"I was tending my ice gardens. To what do I owe this intrusion?" Queen Mavia's voice was strong but brittle, showing little patience.

My father bowed, while my mother stared straight ahead. "I am Alain. It has been many years since I was here last, Great Grandmother."

Mavia studied my parents with a relentless, penetrating stare. They went pale, and I could almost imagine frost forming on their features.

"I know who you are. You have not aged well, Alain. Nor you, Tinaya. What is it that you want? Your time in this room is short."

Mavia's gaze was focused on my parents, but somehow it raised goosebumps on my skin like she was staring straight at me.

My father bowed his head again. "Forgive us for not paying respects sooner. We were trapped for fifteen years in the mines of the Illumined One."

Her eyes flashed a deep blue, and I swore ice began cracking throughout the throne room. Her voice emerged in a thin growl. "How dare that lit-up lizard imprison my kin! I will make my merchants squeeze him for all he is worth. The disrespect he shows me is unconscionable."

Mavia leaned back in her throne with an exasperated huff. "It is a wonder that you survived, considering the weakness of your lineage. How did you find yourself in such a perilous and foolish predicament?"

Fury trickled down my spine. How *dare* she speak to my parents this way.

Mavia's eyes flicked my direction for a fraction of a second. Had she sensed my anger?

My mother muttered something under her breath, but my father gently squeezed her arm. "We were searching for our missing daughter, and we were captured."

My gut wrenched. Fifteen years of their lives, destroyed, because of *me*. I used to be so angry that they never came for me. The hard truth was they couldn't, because they *had* gone looking and wound up trapped in the Realm of Earth.

Bitterness pulled at me. Everything I touched turned to dust.

The queen seemed to be losing interest and started motioning to one of her servants at the back. "Ah. Then how did you escape? Or are you some form of tribute from the Illumined One? I'm not paying anything in exchange for you."

"Our daughter found us. *Rescued* us. We brought her here for an introduction. This is Nevaeh." My father pushed me forward.

Mavia's disinterested eyes narrowed as she turned on me with her icy stare. I was sure she'd been watching me out of the corner of her eye, but now that I had her full attention, I withered a little under the frost of her glare.

"You," she said, clearly unimpressed.

"Me."

She was in front of me before I had time to even draw a breath. Her magic crushed in around me, and I felt the blood drain from my skin.

She snatched my chin in her hand and wrenched my face up to meet her gaze.

"You are a true djinn, though new and weak-spined. Acting like a shy girl of six and hiding behind your parents. That said, I am honestly surprised your lineage produced anything of value. Thin genes. Like tea from a second brewing. I can see it in your hair."

This was the woman who was supposed to help me master my powers?

Screw that.

Rage quaked through my body, and I sucked in a sharp breath. Spark's fire magic erupted from my tattoos, and I smacked her hand away. "Don't touch me."

Ice devils skittered closer along the walls as she hissed in surprise and recoiled from the flames. "Interesting. Fire...and perhaps more spine than I thought."

Her arrogance wormed into me, leaving the taste of bile in my mouth. My rage coiled in my heart, vibrating and ready to explode. I'd heard just about enough.

A quake shook the room.

Did I do that?

Mavia snorted. "You would challenge me in my own palace, little grandchild? That would be foolish beyond reason. You need to cool down and show some respect."

"You need to stop being so rude and earn it."

My parents gasped.

The world pulsed around me, shaking with my anger—as if my fury could melt the palace to the ground.

It welled up inside of me, and I could see it in my mind—the ice collapsing into walls of water, pouring off the islands into the infinite expanse below.

Mavia's eyes widened. "Stop! What are you doing? Control yourself!"

The heck I would. Why should I bend a knee before

this ice-hearted crone? Someone who considered her own offspring—my parents—worthless and unworthy?

My shoulders quaked with anger and—

The roar of waves crashed around me. A hand gently touched my back, and I sucked in a sharp breath of forest air.

For a moment I was somewhere else. A wooded isle at the edge of the sea with gulls crying in the distance. I could taste the salt spray. A place that felt like home. My rage vanished like fire into smoke.

Damian released his fingers from my back, and a pang of longing shot through me. But I could breathe again and *think* again.

Relief rolled through me. The ice palace was still there.

Damian stepped to my side. "We need your help. Your granddaughter needs your help."

"Clearly. She can't control her temper or her magic," the ice queen snapped, desperately trying to regain her composure. "Who are you, anyway?"

I felt Damian's magic flicker, a single pulse that revealed everything. While the strength of her magic was an oppressive cloud, and my own like a wild torrent, Damian's was precise. A sonar ping that shook the hull of a ship. That revealed everything in a single note.

Her eyes dilated, betraying a brief second of confusion.

Damian spoke so low I could barely hear his

response. It wasn't a whisper, but quiet, like a knife hanging at the edge of your throat. "I am an abomination. Help her because I cannot."

The way he said it chilled my flesh. Fearless, threatening, desperate.

She considered us. Her gaze swept over me, peeling me back layer by layer. My eyes dared her to see how far she could go. Finally, she relaxed. "Perhaps I can help. You *are* intriguing, little girl. And I am glad some of my line has borne fruit. What do you need?"

I took a breath, trying to regain my composure. "I became a djinn three days ago. Since then, a demon mage has nearly bound me to his service, and I accidently transported myself to the Realm of Earth with a wish. I need to know how to control my magic and how to avoid getting caught."

Mavia raised her eyebrows and slowly took her throne. "You granted a wish a few days after assuming your true form? That is unusual. The recovery time between wishes is typically much longer, though it becomes faster with age. How did you make the transition in the first place?"

I looked furtively at Damian. "I wished to heal someone."

A knowing smile twitched at the corners of her mouth. She'd clearly caught our quick exchange. "You mean *he* wished for you to heal him. Very noble, *angel*."

Sarcasm dripped from her words.

I shook my head, my frustration returning. "*I* made the wish. He would not."

"Impossible."

"I wished to heal him. It restored an ancient temple at the same time and made plants grow. I don't know how or why."

Mavia leaned forward, and her eyes bored into me, searching for a lie, but found none.

She sucked a sharp breath through her teeth and held it, deciding. "Nevaeh, stay. Everyone else, out. Servants, everyone. Out." She looked pointedly at Damian. "Including you, abomination."

13

Neve

As soon as the room was empty, Mavia slammed the door with a gust of wind and leaned forward on her throne. "You have three questions, then our time is up. No complaining if you don't like my answers."

My brain seized up with a moment of panic. Only three questions? There was so much I desperately needed to know. I had to choose wisely.

I pulled myself up to my full height. "I've never had a chance to learn about my genie powers. How do wishes work and how do I control them?"

She narrowed her eyes. "Technically, that's two questions, but I will let it go this time. Wishes allow you to rewrite reality. If you cannot control your magic, you'll get yourself killed."

I thought of six days ago, when I'd nearly sent an entire bar to hell, and shuddered.

Mavia held up a single finger. "Rule one, you don't have to grant any wishes. Ever. Unless you are bound, that is. Then you are out of luck. Practice resisting. Have people you trust wish for insignificant things and refuse them. It comes with practice."

I crossed my arms. "Great. The first rule of granting wishes is *don't grant wishes.* Check."

Her next finger sprung up. "Rule two. Focus your mind. When someone makes a wish, you'll see a million possibilities. Don't panic. Time will slow so you can choose the right one. Don't rush, be careful. Wishes are entwined with fate and tend to twist themselves. There are always unintended consequences."

I winced. "Like when I had Damian wish that I could speak to my parents, and I got teleported to the Realm of Earth."

"That was because you violated the spirit of rule three—you can't make wishes for yourself."

"Why?"

She pulled out a comb and started brushing her dog's fur. Every stroke made his eyes bug out. "Now that's question two and a very important one. Remember this—genie magic manifests *only in service to others.* As a djinn, you have innate command over the sky and the wind—which is honestly more power than one being deserves. Wishes, on the other hand, call us to improve the world around us, not our own lives."

I mulled it over. "That seems a little unfair."

Her eyes burned, and her hand stopped mid brush. "Unfair? Tell me Nevaeh, what did you *truly* do to deserve your power? Study for decades like an archmage? No. You were born with it. The universe gave you an extraordinary amount of power you did not earn. It's your job to *earn* it."

Her words were like a slap across the face, and I blushed as shame warmed my neck.

Satisfied, she nodded and continued brushing the dog. "Think of it this way. The universe is putting a very large bet on you. It sees someone who can change the world, if only they had the right tools."

I swallowed. That was one heck of a bet.

Mavia rose, placed the dog down on the ground, and gave me an expectant stare. "Now, it's time for Louis's walk. You've got one question left."

Panic lanced me. There was so much I didn't know, and her answers were so obscure. I wanted to ask question after question. How could I choose just one? I had to keep her talking to squeeze out extra information.

"Wait! I'm not sure I understand how the rules work!" I protested.

"Then you have not been listening. Maybe this will clarify what you need to do." The queen stepped forward and spoke with a voice that was quiet, yet overflowing with command. "I *wish* that you would turn into a statue of ice."

My jaw dropped.

Then my magic surged.

Power poured into me, driving the warmth from my body. It was like falling into a frozen lake. I gasped as pain erupted through my feet and fingers. Frost began forming across my clothes and skin, and I stumbled back in shock. My legs were leaden, and I crashed to the ground.

The queen looked on with an impassive expression.

She's trying to kill me with my own magic.

Fear blinded me. I was granting a wish without meaning to. It was the same thing that had happened in the Rift, only stronger. Zara had wished that I go to hell, and I'd nearly transported the entire bar there.

I'd only resisted granting that wish because Damian was there, calming me with his presence and power.

Now, facing down the ice queen, I was on my own.

I summoned my will to resist the wish, but I could barely think with the dread thrashing in my veins.

Pressing my eyes closed, I focused on rejecting the wish, on pushing it out of existence.

Shivers wracked my body, and my thoughts were sluggish. It was almost impossible to imagine that I could be anything but a corpse, frozen over with ice. My arms and legs were too numb to move, and ice crystals spread along my skin.

I would die unless I had warmth.

"Spark," I whispered through chattering teeth.

I am here.

"I need your magic."

It's yours.

I reached out and pulled his fire magic into my body through our bond—as much as I could take. Waves of heat coursed through me. The frost and ice that had covered my skin began to melt away, and the tightness in my chest lessened.

The coldness continued to seep into me, but Spark's magic kept it at bay, and I was warm enough to think. To take control.

Rage and desperation filled me, and I gritted my teeth against the pain of my spasming muscles.

I will resist this wish.

Squeezing my eyes shut, I imagined myself as a statue of ice, melting away, revealing the woman inside. She was furious and strong and bowed before no one, not even a queen.

I pushed back against the wish with all my strength, and finally, it broke.

Relief shook my body, and flames burst from my tattoo.

"How dare you!" I screamed.

The ice queen bared her teeth. "You needed to learn how to control your magic. And you cheated, drawing fire magic from somewhere."

"And what if I had failed? Would you have stepped in?" Exhaustion overwhelmed me, but my emotions felt like a tinderbox ready to explode.

"Why would I do that? If you cannot control your magic, you are a danger to everyone around you. You could kill everyone with an uncontrolled wish. It is not a power for the weak."

Horror streamed through me. Would she really have let me turn into ice? Every part of me wanted to rage but, simultaneously, felt weak.

"You didn't even warn me," I muttered.

"And do you think your enemies will give you warning? No." She pointed her finger at me. "I *wish* that you would turn into stone."

My eyes bugged out in surprise and fury. "You witch!"

My exhausted body suddenly felt heavy, and my skin began to dry. My feet turned white, the color of milky marble, and cracks snaked up my legs. My heart thundered, as I tried to gain control over what was happening.

Queen Mavia moved closer. "Resist the wish. Your fire trick won't help you now."

Focusing my mind inward, I saw a thousand possibilities, each one in which I turned to a statue. Marble. Alabaster. Limestone.

Fear rampaged through my chest, and I frantically pushed the possibilities back, replacing them with an image of me standing whole and defiant in front of the queen.

My fingertips had hardened into stone, but as I focused on that defiant vision, my touch returned and the stone faded, returning to flesh.

The queen nodded, walking a circle around me as I resisted the wish. "You've probably been able to resist weak wishes... words muttered without intention. But it will be much harder to resist an intentioned wish, and harder still to resist one spoken by someone powerful. But at least it appears you can master this."

The pale, marble color slowly faded from my skin and clothes.

Queen Mavia locked my eyes with her gaze. "I wish the flesh would melt from your body."

I reeled back in horror as a thousand images of me melting into a bubbling pile of flesh and bone sprang into my mind.

Pain exploded through my skin, like acid burning it away.

Fighting back the pain, I shoved the images from my head, replacing them with a picture of myself with flawless, airbrushed, magazine-model skin. To be sure. I checked my arms. Still just normal me—but that was good enough.

I snapped my head up to meet her gaze. "You're trying to kill me!"

"No, child. I'm trying to prevent you from getting

killed. Your enemy could try to use a wish to kill you or simply to disorient you in a crucial moment. Imagine what would happen if you were suddenly asked to choose between a thousand possibilities in the heat of battle. You must be prepared."

"I thought you said my friends should wish for insignificant things. Not my death in multiple, gruesome ways."

"I am not your friend. And there's not time to build up to it. But fine, if this tactic is getting old, I *wish* the ceiling of the great hall would collapse and crush everyone within it to death." She bellowed the words through the chamber, and my heart seized.

Damian. Rhia. My parents.

Images of the vaulted ceiling shaking, crumbling, and raining slabs of stone down materialized in my mind. I could see their bodies crushed, twisted, and broken.

"No!" I growled, and with a burst of power I shoved the possibilities away, replacing them with an image of the four of them sitting around one of the great hearths.

Had Mavia just risked crushing her own progeny and servants? She was either confident in my abilities or heartless.

Her expression was like ice.

Probably heartless. And a lunatic.

Queen Mavia nodded impassively. "Well done. You

must be prepared for anything and react fast. Delay could be fatal. I *wish* that—

"No more! I *wish* that you would stop this game!" Power leapt from me, and Mavia stiffened. Her face paled and tensed for a moment, and then relaxed.

She nodded. "Your voice carries impressive weight, young djinn. But I can grant that wish without magic. You did well...after the first two, at least."

My chest heaved. "That was a nasty trick."

"A nasty test. And an essential one. It should be clear now why we keep the nature of our power secret. You may never encounter someone clever enough to use your wishes against you, but my guess is that this demon mage trying to bind you will use every trick in the book."

It was true. I should have seen this was a possibility. Matthias had studied genies enough to learn how to bind them. He might figure out how to use my wishes against me.

My sense of peril was deeper than ever.

But also my confidence. I had felt Mavia's enormous power when she'd commanded those wishes, and yet I'd managed to resist them. There was still a lot to master, but at least I could control whether I granted a wish, and that was one less thing I had to fear. One more decision I could make on my own.

Mavia turned to leave, and I straightened my back. "I have one question left."

She stopped, a smile tugging ever so slightly at the corner of her mouth. "You do."

"How do I stop someone from binding me?"

"Simple. Kill them first. Now, it is far past time for Louis's walk, so I bid you good day, young genie." She nodded and headed toward the door, Louis in tow.

Rage shot through me. She'd just nearly killed me with her wishes, and she put more stake in walking her dog than teaching me about my magic or keeping me alive. This was the answer I needed more than anything.

"That's not enough! I deserve a real answer!" I snapped. Wind whipped around me as my temper rose.

Mavia spun, glaring. "Do you think I am being flippant? You need to face the facts. If someone is trying to bind you, kill them. Binding spells aren't wishes. You can't just resist them. Maybe once you are my age you *might* be powerful enough, but until then, you need to strike fast, without hesitation. If someone is binding you, their intent is to turn you into a servant for a thousand years. That is a fate worse than death."

Her eyes blazed bright blue, and a shiver ran through me. My shoulders dropped. "When Matthias— the demon mage—started casting his binding spell, I felt like he'd drained my power. I felt so helpless. Weak."

Mavia waved a hand in the air. "That is exactly how binding spells work. The incantation will drain your power and use it to bind you to an object. Whoever controls the object will be able to control you. Then they will be able to force you to grant wishes, and there will be no resisting."

"So, what do I do?"

Her gaze softened. "I meant what I said before—kill them. When I was a young djinn, a mage tried to bind me. I ripped the air from his lungs and watched him suffocate to death before my eyes. I have never once regretted it, though sometimes I am haunted by the thought of what would have happened if I'd hesitated. I would be trapped in a bottle somewhere, mad out of my mind."

The horror of that fate raised the hairs on my neck, and I hung my head.

Could I do that?

Maybe. But I'd also made a blood oath to Zara *not* to kill Matthias.

What if she was right? What if killing him was the only way? My freedom or his life. I shuddered. "Sorry. My temper got the best of me. I see now that you were just being direct."

"You need to master your anger. You were completely out of control the first time you challenged me. Luckily, your abomination stepped in or I would have."

Damian. His gentle touch had purged all that anger and emotion in an instant. It was like his touch had transported me to somewhere else, to a place I'd never visited but that my heart longed for more than anything else.

Mavia sighed. "Your temper is part of being a djinn. The fates have gifted our kind with two tools. Righteous anger to rebel against injustice in the world, and through wishes, the power to create change."

I bit my lip. "I guess that makes sense, but it doesn't make it any easier to control."

She sighed. "I will admit, the anger seeps in where it does not belong. That is why I garden."

"You garden?"

"It is the only way I stay sane. Would you like to see? Of course you would." Before I could answer, she rang a bell, and servants poured into the room. "A coat for my guest, and for Louis the sixteenth."

I followed Queen Mavia down a long hall as servants rushed about, bundling me up with a fur coat, mittens, and a round fuzzy hat. I could technically keep myself warm with Spark's magic, but I wasn't about to step on the queen's hospitality.

They bundled Louis up so thickly, I wasn't sure his legs could move. One of the servants carried him as we strode along the hall. An attendant swung a side door open, and we stepped into the bitter air.

My breath caught. Not from the cold, but from the gorgeous sight ahead. A vast garden of ice sculptures stretched before us, glinting in prismatic colors beneath the sun. "It's beautiful."

"I think so. I spend every day in my garden, creating new pieces. It clears my mind."

We descended a flight of shoveled steps and walked along a salted path that wound through the garden.

Rocks were covered with spiky bits of icy snow, like tufts of grass, or porcupines. The ice sculptures were organic, almost plant like.

"They are truly wonderous," I whispered.

"I've had centuries of practice, but then again, I have a natural eye for art."

Louis's legs apparently still worked despite his heavy coat. He bounded through the garden, popping up and down like a ping pong ball.

Mavia gestured to the beautiful sculptures. "If you survive past the next few days, remember this—do something for yourself."

"What do you mean?"

She called a gentle breeze and began shaping fresh snow into a new sculpture. "The ability to grant wishes is our curse. Everyone will know what you can do—that you could make them rich beyond their wildest dreams, or that you could make their problems go away with a flick of the wrist."

She snapped her fingers, and the sculpture exploded in a burst of snow. "You will never be free of it. The incessant begging, the simpering, the judging, the need-ing. You will never know who your true friends are, and who is playing the game. That is why I live here. Alone. Except for Louis and his long line of ancestors."

She looked longingly at the cross-eyed dog rolling in the snow. "He has no idea what I can do. All he wants is love. And treats. But I'm stingy with those, otherwise he'll get fat. Fatter."

It was impossible to be sad in the face of Louis's snow-mad exuberance, but my heart ached for Mavia. So alone.

"You live alone here? What happened to my great-great-great grandfather?"

She fixed me with icy eyes. "I got rid of him. As I told you, everything will change. Your friends, your family, your lovers. They will drain you dry, drop by drop. Every time you grant a wish, you give away a little of your soul. It may not seem like much, or even be noticeable at first. But if you live long enough, you'll start to feel something missing, and you'll always wonder what exactly you gave up."

14

Neve

Mavia didn't talk much the rest of our walk, as if our conversation had drained her completely. Had I taken a little of her soul with all my questions?

How long had it been since she'd simply talked to anyone? She'd probably spoken more openly with me than anyone in a century. Or more.

She was beautiful and cold, a reflection of the ice palace she'd built around herself. That she'd built to keep others out.

Was this my fate, whittled away by the needs of others until all that was left were anger and isolation?

We exited the ice garden, and I shivered, though not from the cold. "Your Majesty, I was wondering if I might ask a favor."

A flock of servants met us at the stairs. One scooped up Louis, while a pair opened the doors.

Mavia turned with an exaggerated sigh. "You're pushing your luck, new djinn. What is it that you need now?"

"I'm returning to Magic Side, but I have a target on my back. Would it be possible for my parents to stay here for a few days until we get rid of the demon and his army? We've been apart for so long. I don't want to put them in harm's way. I have no doubt Matthias would use them to leverage me. They would be safe here..."

Her stare was as cold as ice, and I didn't dare breathe in the intervening silence.

She finally melted, slightly. "Fine. But they're not sharing meals with me. Or conversations."

I smiled. "I think they'll be amenable to that."

The queen nodded, and her servants opened a door into the warmly lit great hall. Mother, father, and Rhiannon sat around a hearth, while Damian leaned against the wall.

I stepped through, but Mavia didn't follow. "This is where I leave you. I wish you the best of luck changing the world. Just don't change it too much."

Not really knowing how I should respond, I bowed. "Thank you so much for your guidance, Your Majesty. I will try to pay you back."

She started to leave but paused. "I can tell you have a warm heart and fierce sense of loyalty, but the world has changed for you, and it will never go back. Trust no one. Your power is the prize in a game that everyone is playing. Friends. Lovers. Enemies. They all want a thin slice of your soul." She looked pointedly at Damian. "Or all of it. Be warned."

Mavia's attendants shut the door soundly.

Damian was at my side in an instant, deep concern blazing in his eyes. "You were gone a while. Did you get what you needed?"

His signature rolled over me, taking me back to that spot along the shore between the forest and the sea. It was all I wanted.

"Yes, I got a little clarity." I measured the man, tracing the lines of his face and body. So strong. So beautiful. So perfect. Would he drain me drop by drop as Mavia had said?

I knew the danger of getting close. Hell, I'd been repeating it over and over in my head since I'd found out he was a FireSoul. He'd hurt me with his lies, yet who was I to call the kettle black? I'd done the same to keep my nature secret.

Damian had always stood by my side and protected me when no one else could, and the truth was, the threat that Damian posed to me no longer seemed so dire. That was becoming more evident the more time we spent together.

Something had changed between us.

My chest constricted at that sudden revelation, and I

turned away, awkwardly shuffling to my parents across the room.

My mother hugged me as if I'd been gone for weeks or years, and I buried my face in her hair, trying to focus on anything but the growing unease in my stomach. "You survived. I was so worried she'd turn you into an ice sculpture and plant you in that horrid garden of hers."

I brushed my mother's hair out of my face and gave her a squeeze. "She's not so bad, once you get to know her."

My mother snorted.

"Where to next?" my father asked.

I grimaced and looked at my mother. "You're not going to like this, but Rhia, Damian, and I are headed back to Magic Side, and I've arranged for the two of you to stay here until we can get rid of Matthias."

Anger streaked my mother's face, and she crossed her arms. "Absolutely not! I haven't survived fifteen years in the Realm of Earth to be entombed in an ice palace! We're coming with you. I've been daydreaming about the different spells I'm going to sling at the man who's causing my daughter so many problems!"

"No. I'm sorry, but it's just too risky. If Matthias hurt you, or found a way to use you against me, I would never forgive myself. Now that I have you back, I'd do anything to protect you. Even spend a thousand years in a genie bottle if that's what it took."

My mother paled but didn't back down. Our argument spiraled around and around like a whirlwind, until we were both exhausted. Luckily, my father dealt the final blow. "I hate it, but Neve's right, dear. In this battle, we're a liability. We need to let her go."

All the fight drained out of my mother as she burst into tears. She held me close as we said our goodbyes.

She dried her eyes. "I can't believe you're leaving us with that *woman*. You owe me decades of lost-daughter time. Mother and daughter margaritas in Cancun, as soon as you're back."

"I have every faith in you. I always knew you would be someone great." My father hugged me tight. "Just remember, we choose our own paths."

Rhiannon pulled us apart, doing the essential best friend duty. "Time to go."

I nodded and watched my parents. My father had chosen a different path than Mavia, and he and my mother were happy. Sure, he wasn't a full djinn like me, but the fact that he'd chosen not to live a life of loneliness and fear had to mean something.

I joined Rhiannon and Damian and took their hands. "Time to go kick Matthias's ass. Where to?"

Damian watched me closely with an expression that was unreadable. "Magic Side. My house. We'll gear up and make a plan."

I closed my eyes and concentrated on Damian's

kitchen, where Rhia and I had kicked back a bottle of wine just a few days ago. It felt like months.

"Goodbye. I love you," I said to my parents, my voice breaking.

The ice palace dissolved as the ether whirled around us, and we shot through the cosmos like a shooting star.

15

———

Neve

My grandmother's words replayed in my head as the ether deposited us in Damian's study: *You'll never know who your true friends are, and who is playing the game.*

I recalled how I'd led my life since I'd lost my parents—alone and afraid of trusting anyone, apart from Rhia.

But my father hadn't chosen that fate, and his voice resounded in my mind: *We choose our own paths.*

Rhia's phone launched into a vibrating fit as text messages flooded in. Where was my phone? I'd given it to her before the wish. I searched the study and found it on Damian's desk, nearly out of battery. I had two missed calls from Zara and several texts.

Where the hells are you? Call me ASAP.

Without bothering to listen to the voicemails, I

dialed Zara and put her on speaker phone. Rhia and Damian huddled around to listen.

"It's about time, Scully. Where have you been?" Zara's voice was tinged with irritation and anxiety.

"Sorry, I was uh..." Damian cast me a sharp look, and I cleared my throat. "Busy, meeting some old acquaintances."

Zara had helped us before, but she was Matthias's daughter. Fates knew she wasn't trustworthy. Even if my grandmother *was* a badass djinn queen, I wouldn't risk Matthias using my parents as leverage.

"Whatever, that's great." Zara said sharply. "Things have escalated after your gig in Apollonia. Matthias is pissed!"

I grinned. Of course he was. We cut the power source he was using to stabilize his new realm.

"Anyways," Zara continued. "I thought you should know that he's made a pact with the underworld lords to draw magic from the hells. Not sure what exactly that entails, but it has to do with powering his new place or something. They've opened some kind of gateway that allows magic and demons to flow through, but he had to weaken the veil to the underworld to do it. Does this make any sense to you?"

My stomach clenched. A pact with the underworld lords and a gateway to the hells. That sounded unbelievably bad. And we'd driven him to it by cutting off his power source at Apollonia.

One step forward, three leaps back.

I tried to calm my voice. "Yeah, that makes some sense. Thanks, Zara, I appreciate the heads up. Anything else?"

"Yup, he's hunting two genies. One is a dao in some catacombs in one of the realms. And the other is, well, *you*. Like I said, he's fucking pissed, and he wants your head, so you better watch out. That's all I've got. Just don't forget our blood oath, Neve." Zara hung up before I could respond.

Rhiannon looked up from her phone. "Blood oath? What did you do?"

"I vowed to not kill Matthias. To bring him in alive."

She sucked wind through her teeth. "Yikes. That might get difficult. What happens if you break the blood oath, and oh, accidently rip the asshole to pieces?"

Damian's jaw clenched, and rage crept into his gravelly voice. "She'll suffer from blood poisoning. Her blood will burn her veins for the rest of her life."

He turned his gaze to me. "No matter the cost, I will not let that happen."

Fates. The way he was looking at me made the blood burn in my veins. I paced the study, keeping my gaze anywhere but on Damian. The tension in him was palpable, and it stoked a fire inside me. I tried to get control of my body, which inexplicably wanted to rage against him and rip off his clothes. Now was not the time.

Grimacing, I rubbed my temples, forcing that image out of my mind before a real-life reenactment followed. "This sounds bad. But does it change our plan?"

"It changes everything about it. If Matthias has made a pact with one of the Lords of Hell, he'll have near infinite resources. An unlimited army. Worse, if he's weakened the veil between the worlds, demons will start slipping through into Magic Side. If it breaks, hell's creatures would have free rein over our world."

Silence filled the room. Rhiannon looked like she was about to throw up, and I didn't blame her. We were paddling upstream of Niagara Falls in a sinking canoe without paddles.

My heartbeat thudded in my ears, and part of me wanted to pack up and planes-walk us all as far away from this shitstorm as possible.

Of course, we couldn't. Magic Side was *my* home, and Matthias needed to be stopped. I'd lived most of my life terrified of people like him and what he was trying to do to me.

No more living in fear.

I straightened my spine. "This doesn't change our plans. We'll need to strike as soon as possible, infiltrate the citadel, and take Matthias out. I don't think your team of assassins is going to be enough. I'll call the Order."

"No," Damian growled. Flames burst down his arms, eliciting a flurry of conflicting emotions in my belly.

"Matthias has opened a gate to hell. This is no longer a war for mortals. We need the help of the Watchers. They're the only ones with the power and numbers to take down Matthias's forces. Reaching an understanding with them is our only viable path forward."

I sucked in a sharp breath.

The Watchers were an almost mythical Order of Angels—dispassionate sentinels that seldom intervened in the world. They were above the laws of the Great Peace that separated humans and Magica, and the only ones with the right to directly intervene in human affairs. They were also known to be ruthless and would do just about anything to restore balance and order, even if that meant unleashing a wave of destruction to accomplish it.

I didn't know the details of Damian's fall from heaven, but afterward, he'd aligned himself with Matthias and fought against them. The Watchers were his sworn enemies and not known for their willingness to forgive.

"Are you certain?" I asked.

Damian looked murderous, and his signature flared, despite his best efforts to contain it. "If the veil between the underworld and earth comes down, the Watchers will get involved, one way or the other. But we need to do it before Magic Side is overrun."

Dread rose in my throat. Going to the angels would be perilous for him. But even with the archmages, the

Order didn't have the resources to battle the unlimited forces of hell.

I took a deep breath. "How do we contact them?"

Damian crossed to the desk in the corner and knelt to open the bottom drawer. "I have a contact in Armenia. I'll go tonight."

"Aren't they your sworn enemies?"

"Yes." Damian closed the drawer and stood, slipping a small black box into his pocket.

"And what will they do when you show up on their doorstep?"

Damian set his jaw.

I shook my head. "Send me. I'll negotiate."

"They won't listen to a mortal, no matter how powerful. They consider you sheep. Shepherds guard sheep but don't negotiate with them."

My anger flared, and a slight wind picked up around me. "Fine, but I am coming with."

"Sorry, Neve, but—"

I grabbed his lapel and pulled him close. "I am coming with. I'm in danger here. You're in danger there. We go *together*. This is not a negotiation, but a statement of the way this is going to happen."

Damian's body tensed. Finally, his lips twitched up at my words. "Fine. Together."

His eyes were deep forests. We were so close that I could feel his heart pounding against my palm. His scent and that ferocious gaze lit an inferno of desire deep in my belly. I lowered my gaze to his lips, and—

"Great! So, we have a plan," Rhia chirped.

I jumped back, heat flooding my face.

She grinned. "You two go make nice with the angels. I'll warn Gretchen about what's going on. If the hells really are about to break open, we'd better beef up security around Magic Side in preparation."

She stood, wrapped her arms around me, and whispered. "You sure you'll be all right without me?"

I squeezed her back. "I'll be fine."

Much to my surprise, I meant it. My stomach churned. Not from fear, but excitement. Whatever darkness Damian had inside him, I was no longer afraid.

Rhia scooped up her jacket and winked at me. "I expect a full report."

Of course she did. I smirked and waved as she left.

Damian watched me closely. "You need food and rest, and I'll need to put a few things in order before we leave."

I shook my head. "We should get going now."

"Absolutely not. After what you've been through in the last day, you need sleep to get your strength back. If you keep pushing past your limits, you're going to become a liability."

Truth.

I was pretty much running on adrenaline alone at this point. That, and hormones.

Damian's butler, Flint, appeared in the doorway. "What would you like for lunch, Miss Cross?"

I narrowed my eyes at Flint and glanced over at Damian, who had sat down at his desk. Either the butler was eavesdropping, or he and Damian communicated via telepathy. My stomach grumbled. "I'll have a cheeseburger if that's on the menu."

"Certainly, Miss Cross. Would you like french fries and a chocolate milkshake with that?" the butler asked.

How did he know I liked chocolate milkshakes with my cheeseburgers? I raised an eyebrow at Damian, but he'd turned to his computer and appeared to be totally engrossed in whatever he was looking at. Convenient.

"Sure, that'd be great. Thanks, Flint."

"Your belongings are still in my room. Make yourself at home," Damian said to me without looking up as Flint disappeared from the room.

Damian was playing this way too cool, like it was no big deal that I'd used his shower and slept in his bed earlier. It made zero sense because since we'd returned from Bulgaria, he'd been doing everything to push me away. I waited another beat, but Damian didn't look up from the monitor.

"Right. I'll see you shortly." I left him to his business and walked down the hall to his bedroom, suddenly feeling exhausted beyond reason.

Closing the door, I shucked off my shoes and ambled to the bathroom. A shower sounded like the best thing since sliced bread right about now. I stripped my clothes and stepped into the shower, letting the hot water ease my tension away.

This felt like heaven.

The only thing missing was Damian. I knew that sounded crazy, but something had changed between us, and I couldn't help it. I picked up Damian's loofah and began scrubbing my body.

He'd said that being close to me made his cravings for my magic more intense. That should have filled me with unease. But the painful truth was that his nearness calmed the frenzy of emotions that had, as of late, threatened to break my mind.

Damian grounded me, and as much as my rational mind had warred against my body, I felt safer with him than anybody else.

Ironically, it was *that* feeling that scared me the most.

I absently scrubbed my body while my mind spun around and around. After about twenty minutes, my skin felt like I'd scraped away my upper epidermis, but my thoughts had finally settled.

Stepping out of the shower, I climbed into a fluffy white robe that was hanging on the back of the door. Because why not?

I brushed my teeth and wrapped my wet hair in a towel, then strolled into Damian's bedroom. It was immaculate, and Rhia's weekender bag was on a wooden suitcase rack beside the armoire. I frowned at it and jumped at the knock on the door.

Fates, for someone who'd recently chosen not to live in fear, I was pretty jumpy. "Yes?"

"Your lunch, Miss Cross." The familiar voice of the butler was muffled through the door. How had he timed that so perfectly?

"Right. Thank you." Adjusting my robe to make sure nothing was peeping out, I opened the door.

The butler was gone. I glanced down at the tray that had been set before the door. A silver, domed plate cover rested beside a fork and knife, a bottle of ketchup, and a crystal glass filled to the brim with chocolatey goodness and a dollop of whipped cream. My stomach roared.

I scooped up the tray, closed the door with my toe, and beelined to the bed. I groaned as I bit into the cheeseburger. This definitely tasted like heaven. After scarfing down lunch, I barely made it under the covers before falling into a food coma.

I was exhausted but safe and full. I could let myself have one moment.

Snuggling into Damian's pillows, I breathed in his scent and drifted off as sleep took hold.

16

———

Damian

I pulled up across the street from Eclipse. In a few hours, there'd be no parking as the city came to life and the bar's patrons filtered in.

Alastair, the Dockside Boss, had texted me that we needed to talk. In person. If he wanted me to pay his men more money, a phone call probably would have sufficed, so it had to be about the attack.

Either way, I was glad to put some physical distance between Neve and me to sort out my mind.

My feelings for her were clouding my judgement, and it was fucking hard to be in the same room without her signature stirring the beast inside of me.

Sliding the keys in my pocket, I crossed to the single black door that was marked with a white circle and the bar's name above it. It was famous, but I'd been there only once for a game of poker in one of the private rooms.

Generally, I kept my business out of Dockside.

The hulking bouncer at the front nodded and opened the door for me. The calmness of his signature indicated that he'd recently shifted.

The space smelled of amber and spice and was warmly lit with no windows. A man was setting up the stage for the evening's show, while another was placing candles on the tables that filled the space.

Clanking bottles drew my attention to the illuminated bar. A woman with a bared midriff was inventorying the rows of liquor bottles stacked three high behind the bar. She spotted me in the mirror and turned.

"I'm here to see Alastair," I said.

"Malek?" She leaned on the bar top and narrowed her eyes. "He's waiting for you in the office."

I followed her gaze to the door with a *No Entry* sign. I nodded thanks and strode over, opening it.

The alpha looked up from a stack of papers on his solid oak desk. "Damian, thank you for coming on such short notice."

His hair was peppered gray, and though his signature displayed the alpha status, he looked more tired than when I'd last seen him. He'd led his pack for several decades. That could grind on you.

One reason I preferred to be a lone wolf, so to speak.

"Alastair." I dipped my head. "Your shifters have proven to be excellent bodyguards. I'll give them a bonus at the end of their contract. What can I do for you?"

"Good to hear, but that's not why I've summoned you. My wolves caught several demons skulking about our warehouse this morning. And I've heard they've been active around Magic Side. Am I correct to assume these creatures are related to why you called in my debt?"

I'd helped Alastair negotiate a trade deal with a pack in Turkey last year. He'd repaid the favor by permitting me to hire six of his best guys for Neve's security detail. The shifters rarely worked with outsiders, but he'd made an exception. They'd be loyal to Alastair, and I knew he wouldn't work with Matthias – a half demon.

"Correct. To be frank, Magic Side is fucked. The veil to the underworld is weakening and demons are slipping through. The Order caught several this morning as well, and they've abducted at least one agent. I'm working on a way to stop this, but it's a long shot."

Alastair leaned forward and narrowed his eyes. "You smell like you're telling the truth, Malek. What the hell is going on?"

I gave him some of the details. Nothing about Neve, though I was certain the security team was feeding him plenty of information. He'd work things out sooner or later.

"I see," Alastair said, after I finished my explanation. "Maybe the pack can help. I don't want the Dens overrun with hell's scum. We've got enough trouble with the demons up in Midway. I'll call a meeting with my council and put my wolves on patrol."

His cellphone vibrated twice, and he answered. "Son." Anger flashed across the alpha's face as he listened, and his eyes turned a honey color as they bore into me. "Hold them. We'll be there in five."

Sliding his chair back, he stood, his irises now back to their normal blue. "Seems like you've got good timing. My son has picked up another two demons, alive this time. How about we take a drive down to the docks?"

Five minutes later, Alastair led me between a series of shipping containers on the old docks. The Dockside pack ran the largest shipping business in the Great Lakes, in addition to their establishments in the Dens.

I hadn't met his son before, but I'd heard he was something of a rogue, preferring to oversee the pack's ventures outside of the city.

We headed for a gray container sitting on a concrete platform. Its doors were splayed open, and a man stepped out, his signature rolled off him in waves and smelling like pine and forest.

The alpha's son.

His signature radiated strength. I cast a side glance

at Alastair, wondering why he permitted his son to match him in power.

"Jaxson, meet Damian Malek. Damian, my son. Show us what you've got."

I dipped my head to Jaxson. "Nice to finally meet you."

He stepped off the container's edge, landing on his feet. He nodded and turned his attention to his father. "Galan and Claire just nabbed four more near Gigi's. I picked up these two in the Flats. They haven't said much."

"I don't expect they will," I said. "Some of them might be informants, but most are slipping through the veil from the underworld. They have no real agenda."

Jaxson's eyes narrowed in on me as a phone rang nearby. "How do we put a stop to that?"

"Malek's working an angle. In the meantime, I'm calling a council to assign shifts around the Dens," Alastair said, climbing into the shipping container and disappearing inside.

A brunette in jeans and a tank top jogged toward us, worry written on her face. "Boss." She stopped beside Jaxson, and her eyes darted inside the container. Her face flushed when she recognized the alpha inside. "Uh, I mean, Jaxson. Claire just called. Reagan's been kidnapped."

"What?" A low growl ripped from Jaxson's throat and his full signature released. "Who took him?"

The wolves froze. He was going to be one hell of a force to be reckoned with once he became alpha.

Alastair strode forward, seemingly unfazed by his son's show of power or by the female wolf's slipup. Perhaps the alpha was preparing to hand over his title soon.

The she-wolf frowned. "Don't know. Some guy. He showed up out of nowhere, grabbed Reagan, and then disappeared."

"What did this guy look like?" I hardly had to ask.

The woman took my measure and glanced at Jaxson before proceeding. He nodded, though I could tell none of them trusted me. "Medium build, dark hair, well-dressed, with thick hipster glasses. Not bad looking, but sketchy as all fuck."

"Matthias." I tightened my fist until my knuckles cracked. Matthias was going to make the wolves pay for protecting Neve. Or use captives as leverage against them. Either way, it was a message.

"What do you know about this fucker?" Jaxson growled.

"More than I'd like. He's our target. I'll do what I can to get your people back."

"What do you need? The pack will help." The rage in his voice made my neck hair stand on end.

I glanced at Alastair who stood stoic. "I need to arrange a few things first. Prepare your pack to double-down on the Dens. I'll be in touch in the morning."

With that, I left.

Now all I had to do was convince the Order of Angels to work with us. Bile rose in the back of my throat. Would they agree?

No doubt, but the cost would be high.

Neve

"Neve." Damian's voice drifted through my mind, a warm and fuzzy feeling.

"Mmmhh." I rolled over and reached out, but my arm flopped onto the empty mattress.

An irrational spark of disappointment panged in my chest.

I peeked an eye open. Damian sat at the foot of the bed in a black long-sleeved shirt with the sleeves rolled up past his forearms. His signature wrapped around me, and I groaned, pulling a pillow over my face. "Were you watching me sleep again?"

"You look so peaceful when you sleep."

Yeah, when I'm not drooling.

I tossed the pillow aside and sat up. Looking down, I

noticed I was still in the bathrobe and naked underneath.

"What time is it?" I said, pulling the collar of the robe closed.

Damian's eyes tracked my movement. "Just after six p.m."

"Six!" I threw the covers off and swung my legs over the bed side. "I thought you only had to put a few things in order."

"I did. But you were sleeping so soundly, I figured our meeting with Nathaniel could wait a few hours."

Leaning forward, I fumbled through Rhia's bag and pulled out some fresh undies—not a thong, thank fates —and a black sweater. Not that the clothes I'd had on earlier were dirty, but I didn't know when I'd have a chance to change again. "Nathaniel, huh?"

Damian was silent, and I knew that conversation was going nowhere.

"An archangel. He was once a brother to me, but I haven't seen him in decades. Not after I gave up on the cause and parted ways with Matthias."

My jaw dropped like a brick. He'd actually offered up information about his past, willingly, without torture. Who was this man?

"Will Nathaniel be open to talking?" I asked.

"He'll likely try to kill me when we show up. But I should be able to strike a deal with him."

A tightness I didn't recognize settled in my chest. I shook my head and stood. Damian was way too calm and collected about all of this.

"*Should* be able to strike a deal? Isn't defeating demons in the best interest of the angels?"

Damian sighed. "The Watchers take their right to interfere in the world very seriously, and are often reticent to act, preferring to let things play out unless there's an emergency."

"But we *have* an emergency. An army of demons is going to invade Magic Side!"

"Magic Side hasn't been invaded yet. The problem will be convincing the Watchers to help us strike first. They may consider whatever is happening in Matthias's Realm of Chaos as outside their jurisdiction."

"That seems short-sighted."

"If it's not already evident from the state of the world around us, angels care little for what is good for people. They're dispassionate Watchers who simply uphold the laws, content to let the world suffer. It was one of the reasons I rebelled so long ago."

What exactly had happened to make him fall? I deeply wanted him to open his past to me. I could feel the rage and regret in his voice, and it drew me to him. I placed my hand on his broad chest, desperate to connect with him and soothe his pain.

His eyes dimmed, dark like the raging sea. They

penetrated straight through me, leaving my soul naked before him. Heat stroked my nerves in a painfully delightful way as his eyes focused on my lips. "Gods be damned, Nevaeh. When you look at me that way, I could lose myself."

My heartbeat skyrocketed. I wanted to push him onto the bed, wrap my legs around him, and sink into his arms. But he tore his gaze from mine and turned toward the door. "We should be on our way."

"Damian." I grabbed his arm, and he stilled.

I didn't want to become like my grandmother—alone and afraid of getting close to anyone. Though I hadn't realized it at the time, embracing my heritage and becoming a full djinn had been the first step in a long and painful process. Choosing to meet Matthias head on and not run was the next step. And this—coming to terms with my feelings for Damian—was the final step. "I made a promise to myself in the Realm of Air."

"Don't say it, Nevaeh." Damian's gravelly voice raked my skin, and fear clenched my chest. Being honest made me vulnerable.

I took an unsteady breath. "I promised that I would stop living my life in fear—of myself, Matthias, and you. I was terrified of my power for so long, but I just had to embrace it. You and I are good together, Damian. I can feel it in my bones. I always have."

Damian's jaw tensed. His eyes blazed, and he stepped back. "I'm sorry Neve, but no matter how much

I want it to be true, we're not good together. Being so close... its torture. Every second, I have to fight back the monster in my soul. If there were any way to change that, I would. I tried with the djinn, but that wish didn't work. He told me I couldn't change what I was—not even with a wish. I don't see a path forward that's safe for us. Once this battle is over, and you're safe, you won't hear from me again. I'm truly sorry, but that's the way it has to be."

His expression had turned to stone. A man alone in the waves, content to drown in the sea.

Hurt, regret, and anger bloomed inside me, and my chest felt like it was splitting open. I swayed as Damian slid his arm free from my grip and walked to the door. He turned back, his stance cold and steady. "I'll be ready in ten minutes. Meet me in the study."

He left, and I stood with my heart collapsing in on itself like a dying star.

I hadn't planned this conversation, but I *had* expected it to go differently. Shit, I'd read everything wrong. I'd let myself think we might actually have a chance.

Straightening my spine, I took a few deep breaths and steadied my emotions. Now was not the time to let them get out of control.

No matter how things turned out with Damian, I would be okay.

What did my heart matter, anyway?

My soul was on the line. My freedom. My life.

I had to fight for that. I had to focus on what mattered. Until this battle was over, I had to be ice.

Ten minutes later, I strolled into the study, collected and calm.

At least, that's what I'd aimed for.

Damian was leaning over his desk, looking at the Atlas of the Planes. Flipping the book closed, he looked up and met my gaze. Something flashed in his eyes. Sadness? Regret?

He rounded the desk and stopped several feet from me. "Ready?"

His shoulders were tense and his eyes dark. A man preparing to lay down his blade and stand before his enemy.

Anxiety settled on me like a smothering cloth. The Watchers were no joke. An order of beings above the laws of both Magica and humankind. Damian's ancient foes. Emotionless and cold, they were known for their ruthless sense of justice.

What would they do to him?

Nothing. Divine power or not, I wouldn't let them.

I stepped forward and took his hands. He flinched ever so slightly but stilled.

Tilting my head, I looked up into his dark green eyes, focusing on a flicker of flame. If we weren't meant to be together, why did this feel so right? Why did my soul call to him?

Circling my waist with his arm, he drew me close. The outlines of the study melted away as a whirlwind of fire dragged us through the cosmos.

18

Damian

We materialized on a rocky plateau enveloped by darkness. Armenia. It had been so long since I'd been here last, I'd almost forgotten the scent of the air and the feel of the monastery's magic.

A cool breeze blew, and the brightness of the moon dulled out the stars, bathing the deep gorge on either side of us in light.

I didn't want to release Neve from my arms. Her jasmine scent intoxicated me, and I could feel her heart pounding against my chest.

Regret tore at me as I pulled away and turned toward the monastery perched on the edge of the plateau, burying the ache that filled my chest after our earlier conversation.

Neve had convinced herself that we were good for each other. That we might have a fighting chance.

Delusions.

This was my fault. I had played with fire, and now she was the one getting burned. I should have been cold from the start. I should have kept my own desires in check. Clearly, I had just as little control over myself as I had over my FireSoul craving.

That was perilous.

I'd tried to warn her. She knew well enough what I was capable of, that I was a gods damned monster. Even now, I struggled with my desire for her magic.

She shouldn't have let her guard down so easily.

Anger seeped into my veins, and I silently cursed the pitiless fates.

The outlines of the monastery walls were visible, and a single light glowed in one of the towers.

"Are you ready for this?" Neve appeared by my side, and I fought the urge to look at her.

I'd never be ready for this, but it was necessary.

"When I fell, I felt betrayed. By the gods, by my brothers, and by Nathaniel. I spent half a century making them —*him*—pay by waging a war to bring everything they stood for down. I didn't see it at the time because I was blinded by my rage, but I'd become what I hated most."

The words flowed from my mouth. There were no excuses for what I'd done, only regret, though that was dulled by the hollowness that now filled my soul. I'd never been so open with anyone.

Neve took my hand, weaving her fingers through mine. "Our past might forge us into what we are now, but it doesn't dictate our future, Damian."

She squeezed my hand then slipped away and headed toward the monastery.

If only that were true for me.

We picked our way through the grass that covered the rocky plateau. A gentle hum vibrated through the air, along with the scent of pomegranates. The distant echo of bells that I'd known intimately. Once.

I reached for Neve's arm, gently tugging her to a stop. The vibration grew and swept around us like an eddy, and Neve palmed the khanjar at her hip.

A gush of air pummeled into us, and then a deafening explosion split the sky. A glowing form crashed into the ground ten feet ahead, releasing a shockwave that rocked the ground. I steadied Neve, blocking her with my body.

"Holy mother of gods," Neve whispered as she peered around my shoulder.

"Not quite, child. But I appreciate the sentiment."

Steeling myself, I met the icy gaze of Nathaniel. Archangel, brother, enemy. The aura of white light that cascaded around him was radiant. Blinding.

Once, I had been the same.

"Damian." His voice rumbled through the air like

distant thunder. Apart from his clothes, he appeared the same, even his arrogant smile. "What has it been, sixty years? I vowed to kill you if we ever crossed paths again. Why are you here?"

Age-old bitterness and fury surfaced, and I clenched my fists as flames licked down my palms. "Try. If you must. But that's not why I'm here. I've come to make a deal, Nathaniel. With the Order of Angels."

The words twisted in my gut. *I can't believe I'm fucking doing this.*

The angel's eyes rounded, and the corner of his lips pulled up. "A deal? Now what could you possibly offer us?"

He stepped forward, his footsteps cracking the earth beneath. My magic flared, and flames erupted around me. "A chance to do good in the world, rather than to sit idly by and watch it burn down around you."

Nathaniel stopped and narrowed his eyes at the flames rising from my skin. "You need help, brother."

"True, but so do the angels."

His eyes burned with radiant light but betrayed no emotion. "Speak."

"Matthias is hellbent on bringing down the angels."

"Matthias," he growled. "That has *always* been his desire, and yours as I recall." Nathaniel's voice cut through the air like a whip.

"The game has changed. Matthias has created a new plane—a Realm of Chaos—as if he were one of the creators himself. To power his spells, he's struck a deal with a lord of one of the hells and is amassing an army of demons. The veil will break soon and when it does, the hells will open, and chaos will follow."

Nathaniel's expression hardened and his aura flared. "How is this possible?"

"Through wishes. He has two genies. Soon to be three," Neve said calmly, appearing at my side. "We don't have much time."

"Genies. Like you, child?" Nathaniel's voice boomed, echoing through the gorge. His gaze locked onto Neve, and I ground my teeth against the instinct to protect her.

It was a foolish instinct. She was a full djinn with powers now far surpassing my own. Yet the urge irrationally remained.

Neve was silent, and Nathaniel shifted his eyes to mine. "What do you propose, fallen?"

"You help us invade Matthias's citadel and close the gateway to the hells. That will cut off his source of power and prevent him from mustering an army."

Nathaniel considered us with piercing eyes, then shook his head. "I'm sorry but no. I understand your position, but this conflict is not within our jurisdiction. *Yet*. We do appreciate you bringing this information to us. It is a step in the right direction, and demonstrates that you may yet be redeemed, Damian."

I opened my mouth, but Neve snapped. "What do you mean, not in your jurisdiction? Matthias is planning to invade our world. That seems pretty damn relevant."

Nathaniel glared at her. "There are rules. We do not interfere in the hells, and they do not interfere here. That is the way we keep the fragile peace. If Matthias attacks Magic Side, we will fight, with or without you."

Neve tensed. Her signature swelled, and the breeze picked up. "Isn't it *your* job, angel, to watch over Earth? Well, newsflash, you're doing a shit job of it. Demons are already slipping through the veil in Magic Side. The invasion has started."

She took a step forward, and I tried to stop her, but she pulled away and continued. "What will the gods say when the veil breaks entirely and you've done nothing?"

I coiled my muscles and prepared to block Nathaniel if he moved for her.

But he didn't. He watched her closely, then spoke. "You're brave for one so young. I'll attribute your insolence to your newly acquired powers."

Wind tore at the hillside, and white lightning flashed in Neve's eyes. Her voice boomed through the hills. "And you're a fool, for one who's lived so long. You have the power to prevent tragedy. If you don't act, you're as guilty as Matthias."

"You are not listening," Nathaniel growled. "This conflict is outside our domain. We have a treaty with the underworlds that we will not break."

Rage poured off Neve like rain from the heavens.

"I'm listening to you hide behind rules. I don't know what your little treaty entails, but I do know the Realm of Chaos didn't exist when you made your deal with the devils. It's neither the domain of the angels or demons, but a new world created by genie magic. If you insist on doing nothing, it will become just another extension of the underworld. One with an open portal into Earth. Do you really want to be the one who refused to shut the gates when the armies of hell arrived?"

Nathaniel gritted his teeth and fixed Neve with a relentless stare. Finally, he spoke. "Perhaps you are right. This realm is neither part of Earth nor part of the hells. We might be permitted to help close the gateway, to ensure its neutrality."

"I'm glad you're willing to do the bare minimum to ensure human safety," Neve hissed, venom palpable in her voice.

Nathaniel wasn't listening. He had tilted his head toward the heavens and closed his eyes, using telepathy to communicate with the Order of Angels.

The howling wind died as we waited.

"I can see why you left," Neve said through the side of her mouth.

I nodded.

Finally, Nathaniel lowered his head and opened his eyes. "It is decided. The angels will help with two conditions. Damian, you betrayed us and have remained a thorn in our side for centuries. There is little trust for either of you amongst the Watchers. Before we progress any further, *both* of you will make a binding oath that you will forgo giving aid or support to demons in the future."

He narrowed his eyes on Neve, and she flinched. " Fine," she said.

"I also agree."

"Good," Nathaniel said. "Then you will sign that first."

The air cracked and a glowing document and feathered pen appeared in Nathaniel's hands. He strode forward and handed me both, the ground shifting under him. I read over the oath, signed my name, and handed it to Neve.

She read it closely, biting her lower lip before locking eyes with Nathaniel. "The wording of this is unclear. I have a few friends who are part demon, and I'm not giving them up."

I fought back a smile as a low rumble burst from Nathaniel's chest, and his eyes glowed white hot. "Where did you find this one, Damian?"

"She makes a point. If the document is unclear, how can we be expected to follow it?"

Nathaniel snatched the oath and pen, scratching out the line and scribbling some words under it, before handing it back to Neve.

She examined the oath and frowned. "Not much better, but it'll do."

Another rumble erupted from Nathaniel, but he said nothing. After signing it, she handed the oath and pen to him.

"What is the second condition?" I asked.

He slipped both into his trouser pocket and met my gaze, a smile forming on his lips. "You, Damian, must stand before the Assembly and atone for your crimes."

Neve's eyes flashed, and the wind rose again. "What does that even mean?"

"Judgement. Punishment."

She growled and shot forward, the wind howling around her. I caught her and pulled her back. "It will be fine. I was prepared for this," I whispered.

She glared, shooting daggers with her eyes. "Don't you dare agree to anything before you know what the limits of their judgement will be. I'm not letting them lock you away. I'm not letting them hurt you. I can't lose you."

Her heartbeat pounded against my chest, and I breathed in her scent before releasing her and turning to Nathaniel. "I agree."

"Damian!" Neve shouted.

"We must all atone for our sins, child. The gods seek retribution but that does not mean they are without mercy."

A lie.

I could feel the anger vibrating in her signature. Nathaniel met her eyes with a cold stare.

Finally, the slightest amount of tension left her shoulders, thank fates. The angels might be the guardians of this world, but they were vengeful and dangerous, especially when crossed.

I knew that all too well.

19

Neve

I focused my lingering anger on the back of Nathaniel's perfect head as Damian and I followed him down the slope to the monastery.

Somehow, I had mastered my rage long enough to get my message across. That had felt good. I didn't expect that angels took kindly to threats, and I wasn't entirely sure I could rip them down out of the sky, but I would sure as heck try if they hurt Damian in any way.

But that wasn't the message I wanted to send. They had to know he had changed. To see the good that I knew was there.

Would they care?

The ground was rocky and covered in tall grass, so I had to pick my way carefully to avoid face planting. Damian and Nathaniel seemed unfazed by the terrain, and every step the angel took was followed by a low, ominous boom.

If Rhiannon were here, she'd joke about his weight.

Actually, it was more likely she'd make a comment about his butt. *That girl.*

Nathaniel was gorgeous like Damian, in a cold, all-too-perfect angelic kind of way. He was also massively built, but not like a giant.

Sandy blond hair, blue eyes, and a dimple in his chin. But his personality was a buzz kill, and I wanted to slap the condescending smile that graced his face.

Damian gently touched my arm and nodded. Was that supposed to be reassuring?

Well, it wasn't.

I didn't like this plan, and I had zero trust in the angels. If they threatened one hair on his head, I would turn into a cyclone and grind this whole place into the ground.

Angels or not, good luck trying to fly in a hundred and sixty mile-an-hour wind. Assholes.

I steadied my thoughts. *Keep it together, Neve.*

The stone walls of the monastery rose in the darkness, and we entered through an arched gate. The ground was level and free of rocks, and I couldn't help but be awed by the beauty of the place. The whole complex was surrounded by a fortified wall with several towers.

Nathaniel led us toward a church that held a

commanding position over the valley below. Like all the structures here, the church was constructed from hewn stone. The air inside was cool, and a light breeze blew through the narrow windows. Candles were set along the altar, and their light danced across the space, illuminating the tall central dome.

Nathaniel stopped and turned to me. "This is as far as you go, child."

My irritation swelled. "I'm not a child, so please stop calling me one. And no, I'm coming with."

Nathaniel met my eyes with a cold stare. "You are in our domain, now. You must obey our laws."

I stepped up, so that only mere inches separated us. "And when you fly, angel, you are in mine. If you harm Damian in any way, I will make you wish you had never learned to crawl, let alone taken to wing. I will make you wish your eyes had never seen the sky. I'm holding you accountable for anything that happens, and I will have my own justice."

My voice was little more than a whisper, yet it rumbled like thunder. The wind rose, and it was as if the candle flames bowed before me.

Nathaniel's expression was impossibly impassive, but his body was tense, and he was struggling to stand, like the whole weight of the heavens were bearing down on him.

But I knew this wasn't the way to negotiate with angels.

I steadied my breathing and pushed the rage from my heart. "If I can't enter, so be it. Carry my words to your assembly. I have witnessed who Damian is. Whatever atoning needed to be done, it has already happened. He's put his life on the line to protect me and people he has never met. He has my faith. We are here to defeat Matthias, so help us do it."

Finally, after a long pause, Nathaniel spoke. "I hear the truth of your words, and I promise to take them to the angels. I will speak upon Damian's behalf."

Sorrow and pain filled Damian's eyes. Why was he looking at me that way? Like this might be the last time he laid eyes on me.

Panic and protectiveness surged inside me, and a barrier of wind burst around us, shielding us from Nathaniel.

I turned to Damian. "Why do I feel like you won't be coming back from this?"

He was silent, but the anguish and regret that cut his face was an answer in and of itself.

"Damian, don't do this. There has to be another way." My voice sounded ragged, and my chest heaved.

I couldn't lose him.

Damian placed his hands on my shoulders and locked me with those brilliant green eyes. His magic washed over me, calming my tumultuous emotions. "It will be okay, I promise."

His words wrapped around me, and I took a breath and nodded.

Why did my heart still trust this man after all his lies?

But there was nothing else I could do.

The wind wall dropped as I released my magic, and Damian walked with Nathaniel to the altar.

A thunderclap ripped through the space, and I doubled over, clutching my hands over my ears. The faint rustle of the breeze returned, and I looked up.

Nathaniel and Damian were gone.

All that was left was the ringing in my ears and the ache in my heart.

~

Damian

Nathaniel and I walked down a white marble hall illuminated by a thousand candles.

We were no longer on Earth, but in a gateway to the heavens.

A darkness had settled over me as I steeled myself for what was next. I knew the consequences when I took up the sword against the angels. I'd run from them for so many years, but now that it was time to face them, it mattered not.

Neve's words from earlier resounded in my head, driving me to the brink of insanity.

You and I are good together.

We would not be together. Not in this world or the next.

Unbearable pain spread through my chest, and my dragon reared up in a desperate plea. Even though Neve was on Earth and I in heaven, the beast still craved her magic.

Bile rose in my throat, and I grimaced.

I was an unstoppable monster that needed to be put down. I measured Nathaniel's vacant, stoic expression. I might get my wish, momentarily. In the end, perhaps it was the best way to keep Neve safe.

"A penny for your thoughts, Damian," Nathaniel said.

I glared at him. "A favor."

Nathaniel gave me an inquisitive look.

"You owe me nothing, but I ask one thing of you, brother. Protect her. No matter what happens."

"Have you learned nothing in your time on Earth?" He smiled. "The angels do not meddle in the affairs of mortals. A canon you should have heeded."

I bit back my anger, focusing on the pain in my chest, as we approached a large room lit by hanging braziers.

The Assembly.

Memories bombarded me as I stepped into the circular space. The assembly of Watchers sat on the tiered benches that encircled the room.

Nathaniel veered left, and I strode to the podium in the center. I knew the trial protocol. Questions, judgement, and atonement. This would all be over soon if they met my conditions.

"Damian Malek. Once one of us, now a criminal. We are pleased that you have returned to make amends for your crimes," an archangel to my right said.

Kushiel. Of course.

"I didn't come here to atone for my sins. I came here as part of a deal." I cast a cold glance at Nathaniel, who nodded.

"So we have been told." Kushiel's long, dark hair draped around his face, and his eyes blazed with wrath. "We have deliberated and come to a decision."

It had better be the fucking right decision, or I would unleash hellfire on these pompous bastards.

"The Order of Angels agrees to assist in the battle against Matthias and his legion on two conditions," the archangel said. "First, you will swear an oath of fealty to the Watchers.

An oath of fealty meant they wouldn't kill me. That was something, at least.

The second condition could mean only one thing— I'd be stripped of everything.

"Secondly, you must accept the punishment that we have decided appropriate for your crimes." Kushiel circled the room slowly. "You will forfeit your angelic powers. If you agree to both conditions, we will align with you."

My heart stilled as the air left my lungs. I'd assumed they'd strip all of my magic, but the notion of losing only my angelic half was gut wrenching. Even tainted by my fall and by my rage, it was the better half, after all.

"Can you take my FireSoul magic?" It was worth a shot.

Murmurs echoed through the room, and Kushiel smiled broadly. "That is not the agreement. You have rejected the righteous path of the angels. You must relinquish those powers."

Could I live without my dark angel magic? My innate healing. My wings. Forever earthbound. My dragon roared in my chest and flames arced around me, eliciting several gasps from the angels.

If it meant that Neve would live a life of freedom, I'd give up everything. "I agree to your conditions. But Matthias is mine, I will deal with him."

Kushiel leaned forward. "Matthias is ours to judge and to punish. We fought him when you were his ally. He will endure our justice. That is non-negotiable."

I nodded. Vengeance did not matter. My magic did not matter. My life did not matter.

The only thing that mattered was protecting Neve from him.

I would have accepted any deal they offered.

A parchment and pen materialized on the podium.

Gold script outlined the oath of allegiance to the Order of Angels. The irony tore at me as I picked up the pen and paused, recalling the years I'd spent at war, only to align with them with a few strokes of a pen. It was infuriating, and I grimaced at the thought of the gods laughing.

But I had a dead hand, and it was time to fold.

I signed the oath, and both it and the pen vanished in a twist of smoke.

Kushiel spread his arms wide and smiled. "In the years that I've known you, Damian, I never thought it would come to this. I must say how delightful it is to be surprised, even if it is once a millennium."

He gestured to the seated angels around us, and they stood in unison. A silence fell over the room, and Nathaniel appeared at my side. "Brace yourself, brother."

The djinn had stripped me of my FireSoul magic, if only for a time. The pain had been unbearable.

It didn't matter.

Stepping away from the podium, I took position in the center of the room, forcing the tension from my body.

Reaching into my pocket, I retrieved a box with the necklace—a golden starburst pendant on a chain. I hadn't worn it since my fall, but I'd kept it for some reason. Now that I was giving up my dark angel, it seemed silly to keep such a token. "I give up my angel."

I tossed the box to Nathaniel, who caught it and peered inside. He met my gaze and nodded solemnly.

I closed my eyes as a rising cacophony of bells filled the room. The sound wrapped around me, vibrating in my bones and piercing my ears as it grew to excruciating decibels.

And then it stopped.

I opened my eyes. The angels began filing out of the room, one after the other, until it was just Nathaniel and me.

I turned to the angel. "I don't understand. Why have they left?"

"It is done, Damian. You've atoned and are now free to go," he said.

Confusion pulled at the corners of my mind. I summoned my wings, but nothing happened. Turning inward, I searched for the dark angel that certainly still had to be there because...I'd felt nothing. But it was gone, too. Only a deep, oppressive hollow remained.

Sorrow sunk into my bones. I was a mere mortal now. Bound to the Earth and subject to its laws.

"You were expecting a more dramatic transformation? Often, the greatest changes are subtle. Silent. We do not even notice them. I am sure you have no idea how much you have changed since we last stood, face to face, so long ago."

I nodded, stunned.

"As to our part of the bargain, we will help you close

the gateway to hell in the Realm of Chaos. You have a way in?" Nathaniel asked.

I flexed my fist, the absence of my dark angel magic so strange. "Yes. We have access through a teleportation circle in his tower. We should use small teams and move fast. Take out Matthias. Destroy the gateway."

"And when can you be ready to strike?"

"Give us till dawn. Chicago time."

We clasped arms. "Agreed. I'll pull together a team of angels. You had better get back to your djinn. She is waiting and wracked with worry."

At the mention of her, the dragon thundered in my chest, louder than ever before, and flames erupted around me. Acid burned my throat. I couldn't be around her. My cravings were now unchecked, and I might not be able to curb them. "I need you to do something for me, Nathaniel. And don't fucking tell me you can't."

The angel's eyes glimmered as he pulled back from the flames.

"I beg you now, as an ally of the Watchers. Protect Neve. You've taken the only part of me that has kept my cravings for her magic in check. I'm only a FireSoul now. A monster, and I..." The words stung as they came out because they were the truth. "I will kill her."

Nathaniel shook his head. "I very much doubt that."

Flames flicked up my arms as frost formed on my clenched fists. "You have no idea the strength it takes to master the dragon within me. It's ravenous. Its lust for power cannot be quenched. The things I've done… there's a reason FireSouls are hunted. They are murderers and thieves. Eventually, inevitably, I will succumb to my craving for her magic."

He placed his hand on my shoulder. "Is power what you crave?"

"Yes. Since the dawn of my life."

He studied my face, long and hard. "I think not."

"It's true. A deafening roar of desire is in my soul. I have killed for it before."

Nathaniel drew close "And do you desire to kill me and seize my power?"

"No."

He chuckled. "You are, more than any man I know, a prisoner of your past. And a fool, Damian. You've become so accustomed to lying, that I fear you can no longer see the truth, even when it is so glaringly obvious."

I ground my teeth and growled. "And what truth is that?"

The angel stared at me blankly. "You do not crave power. Fates, you willingly gave up your angel—*the most powerful part of you*—to protect Nevaeh. You do not crave magic. You crave *her*. It is as clear as day."

The candlelit hall slanted, and I careened into the wall as nausea rolled over me. "That can't be."

My dragon roared.

"If you only craved her power, then you would have

killed her long ago. Yet, you've fallen on your knees before your enemies. You've given up your magic. You've fought for her, every step of the way. Tell me, when have you done that for anyone?"

It wasn't possible.

I had slain the efreet for its powers.

But only to protect her.

I had ripped the soul from an ice devil.

To protect her.

I dragged a hand through my hair and focused on the woman who left me so conflicted. The dragon surged within, and emotion tore through me. Protectiveness, admiration, desire.

Gods. I had fallen for her.

"Take some time to consider this, but not too long. The girl is waiting." Nathaniel's eyes glinted and he turned, leaving me. "We'll meet you in Magic Side at dawn."

With that, the angel disappeared, leaving me alone with the dragon, who desired only one thing in the world.

20

Neve

The wind sang through the valley below, and fiery pink hues streaked the sky.

Where the heck was Damian?

I released my breath as I paced outside the church. It had been too claustrophobic inside, and I needed fresh air to get control over my emotions. I'd decided to wait calmly for thirty minutes, but then when the two angels didn't show, my temper flared, and I'd almost blown the basilica down.

That certainly wouldn't have put me on good terms with the gods or the angels, I snickered.

Screw them.

It had now been an hour since Damian had left with that smug angel, Nathaniel. *Bastard.* I should have demanded that they take me with. What if he were in trouble or worse?

My heart sank, and I grasped my chest.

No. Damian knew what he was doing. He wouldn't be so stupid as to put his life in danger.

I shivered against the cool dawn air. Shit. How long was I supposed to wait, and what if he didn't return? I could planes-walk back home again, so at least I wasn't stuck. But I couldn't leave Damian. *I wouldn't.*

A gust tousled my hair, and goosebumps prickled my skin. I swore I detected the faintest traces of pine, sandalwood, and...

My breath hitched, and I ran to the church's entrance.

Damian stood on the front step, bathed in a brilliant glow I'd never seen around him before. Like he'd been...reborn.

Shaking the thought from my mind, I ran toward him and launched into his arms. He pulled me close, and as I wrapped my legs around him, all the world's troubles dimmed. "What took you so long?" I whispered.

"Making deals with the angels. They agreed to help." He brushed his cheek against mine, and my body quaked with need.

Pulling myself back, I looked up into his forest green eyes. Something about him had changed. The shadows were gone, and he seemed at ease. "What's happened? You're...different. What did they do to you?"

He traced his thumb along the line of my jaw. "They made me see clearly for the first time in a long while."

The shield he'd erected against the world was gone. It was like I was seeing the real Damian for the first time. He was radiant, gorgeous.

His fingers wound into my hair as he dragged his gaze to my lips. Heat burned through me, and I pulled his mouth to me. His tongue parted my lips, sweeping across mine.

White hot desire cascaded through me, and more than anything in the world, I needed him, around me, on me, in me.

Squeezing my ankles together, I pushed against him, feeling the heat rise between us. Resting his hand on my jaw, he pulled his lips away. "Not here. Let me take you somewhere."

My chest heaved as I sucked in air and nodded. Gods, I didn't care where we were as long as this happened.

The ether swirled around us. Damian was planes-walking us, but where? I pressed my face into his chest as the cosmos spun. Flames washed over me, and then the spinning stopped.

Damian set me down.

We stood on a steep cliff overlooking the sea, surrounded by tall trees that disappeared into the fog. I could taste the salt spray and smell the ancient pines that pressed close. The air was damp, as if rain were about to fall.

The misty forest was silent—except for the gentle crashing of the waves and the soft cry of gulls.

I stepped back from the precipice. "Where are we?"

"My cabin. A retreat from the city."

Something about this place strangely felt like home. I took a deep breath, inhaling the scents and sounds. "This place is you. It feels like you."

Damian smiled and brushed the hair from my face. "Funny. Something about it makes me think of you. I've been wanting to bring you here for a while. But there's been no time. The world's always been—"

I place my fingers to his mouth. "We have time now. For a second, the world doesn't matter. Don't spoil the moment."

He took my hand and pulled me toward a large cabin nestled in the trees. "I wouldn't dare."

We slipped through the door into the dark cabin. With a quick wave of his hand, a fireplace and a dozen candles burst to life. I drew my gaze over the white sheepskin rug in front of the fire, settling my eyes on the wooden sleigh bed.

I smiled. "You're just full of surprises, Mr. Malek."

"No more surprises, Miss Cross." He closed the distance between us, his gaze burning into mine. "From now on, you'll know all my secrets."

Heat returned, chasing away the cold. My legs quaked as he cupped the back of my head and lowered his mouth to mine. Before his lips landed, he paused.

"What changed?" My words were barely audible, as I struggled to stand. "You're no longer afraid to be close."

"I finally realized what my dragon was trying to tell me all along. You are my treasure and always have been. The one thing my soul couldn't live without."

His voice was like honey, and my heart ached at his words. If I hadn't been dizzy with desire, I might have worried that it would explode. I licked my lips, and his eyes followed the movement. "What are you waiting for then?"

"I plan on taking my time with you, Miss Cross." He traced his thumb over my lips and smiled.

My heartbeat thundered in my chest, and my whole body ached to make contact with his. Gods, I didn't know how much longer I could wait—

And then he pressed his mouth to mine. Our arms wound around each other and our bodies became one as we kissed like this would be our last.

Because it could very well be.

Every movement of his hands, every tug of his mouth was overshadowed by one truth—that there might be no coming back from the battle ahead. That this might be my last moment of freedom.

But none of that mattered, because all that I wanted

and all that I needed was Damian. And finally, I had him.

My back crashed into a wall. I pulled my lips from his and yanked my sweater off. He planted his palms behind me, and flames danced in his eyes as he drew his gaze down my body.

"You're beautiful," he whispered.

Grabbing the hem of his shirt, I drew it over his head. *He* was beautiful. I traced the outlines of his muscles, dragging my fingers slowly down to the top of his pants.

His heart pounded beneath my touch, and his pupils flared with desire as he unbuttoned my jeans and dragged them down. He planted light kisses along my neck, and I gasped as his fingers slid down my side, leaving a trail of goosebumps.

Slipping his hand under my panties, we both moaned when his fingers found my center. Pleasure mounted as he worked my heat, and I rocked my hips against his hand, desperate for the release. It wouldn't take long. He touched me like he knew my every need.

My head tilted back, and my legs gave way as pleasure rippled through me.

I collapsed into Damian's arms, and he kissed me softly.

I traced his arm with my fingers, wanting to savor the moment—but I had words that needed to be said.

Pushing back in his arms, I met his eyes. "After we defeat Matthias, I want you to stay. With me."

Damian smiled and kissed my neck, burying his face in my hair. He whispered softly, "I'm not going anywhere. I'll always be by your side if you want me."

My heart felt like it was going to climb out of my chest. I pulled him close. "I do want you."

He kissed me again and lifted me up, his hardness pressing against me. Desire pooled in my center as I wrapped my legs around his waist. Feeling the slickness between my thighs, I ground my hips into him. "I want you Damian, all of you, right now."

He growled and carried me over to the sheepskin rug beside the fireplace. Gently lowering me onto the soft fur, he kissed my chest, then dragged his mouth down my stomach, grazing my skin with his teeth. Shudders racked my body when his mouth found the apex of my thighs. My back arched, and I panted, trying to draw in air. Desire grew but I wanted—*needed*—more.

"Damian, please," I pulled him away before it went too far and fumbled with the button on his pants. "I'm clean and on birth control, and I need all of you."

His eyes flashed with primal desire, and he quickly removed his pants. I could barely control my breathing. I gave myself one moment to trail my eyes down his gorgeous body, and then I pulled him down on top of me. He slowly buried himself into me, and I screamed at the tightness and pleasure of it.

Pure bliss like I'd never felt before blossomed as we melded into one another, desperate to remove any distance that had once separated us. Before I lost it, I rolled him onto his back and climbed on top. We breathed as one, and it didn't take long to find the perfect rhythm.

As we moved together, our signatures and souls entwined, and everything around us faded away. Desire grew and before I knew it, he pushed me over the brink of ecstasy. I quaked as pleasure pulsed through me, and after the cascade had left my body, I slid off him and lay at his side.

The candlelight flickered on the walls, as I traced my fingers along his chest.

His hand found mine. "I love you. I'm sorry it took so long to see."

My heart stopped.

We hadn't been together long. Weeks, really. But my soul knew the truth. Damian was the one.

"I love you, too." I interlaced my fingers with his and laid my head on his chest, feeling more content than ever in my life.

21

Neve

We returned to Damian's house at dawn.

I was barely functional. There'd been a lot of activity and not a lot of sleep. We probably should have gotten more rest before facing the end of the world, but if this was the end, I didn't regret it for a second.

Coffee would fix everything.

I took a deep breath and leaned against the railing of Damian's deck. The windows of the skyrises across the channel shone with golden light, and reflections danced on the unusually placid waters of Lake Michigan. The air was still. The calm before the storm.

Damian joined me and passed over a piping hot double-espresso. "Jet fuel?"

I sipped it. "Nectar of the gods."

He leaned on the railing and set his jaw, brooding on

the task ahead. I shifted my hand along the rail, so that it pressed gently against his.

After a quiet moment, he sighed and shook his head, as if waking from a dream. He smiled. "How do you want to do this?"

I took a sip of the strong brew. "I was kind of hoping this moment wouldn't come, but I'm not gonna be able to breathe until Matthias is under lock and key and we've closed the gateway to hell."

He moved his hand on top of mine. "Agreed. So, what's our plan? Take out Matthias first or the portal?"

I ground my teeth. "There's nothing I'd like better than taking that bastard out. But the portal has to be our priority. The longer it's open, the weaker the veil between the worlds will get. We've got to shut it fast before demons pour through Matthias's realm into ours."

"So how do we shut it?"

"Ethan is going to teach me an incantation to disable the spell that is keeping the portal open. Unfortunately, any spells that are strong enough to hold open a gateway to hell are going to take a ton of power to break. My magic has grown a lot over the last week. Hopefully, it's enough."

Ethan was an archmage from the Hall of Inquiry. He'd helped me seal the Archives when they'd flooded and given us the spell book to banish the marid.

Damian frowned. "That's a lot of guessing."

"Honestly, it's going to be a shitshow. As soon as we start sealing the gateway, Matthias will know, and he'll show up with his genies and all the forces of hell. We're going to be overrun."

Damian rubbed the back of his neck. "I'm not sure we can handle that all at once. We need to divide and conquer. You take the angels and shut down the portal. I'll take a strike team and try to disarm Matthias before he has time to react. Even if I fail and he escapes, I can buy you time."

I saw what Damian was doing and pushed back. "No way. That *bastard* is mine."

Flames flickered down his arms, and I could feel the tension in his body. "Matthias has nearly bound you twice. He can drain your power, like kryptonite."

I tightened my fists as my anger rose. "Matthias has haunted my life. He's like the sword of Damocles hanging over my head. I need to be the one who brings him in."

Damian hung his head. "I know. I can't lose you to that *bastard*, but I believe in you. You've done things I never imagined possible. This is your call."

I clenched my jaw as frustration tore through me. I knew I could defeat Matthias. I'd suffocate him, as the queen had done to the mage that had tried to bind her.

But I couldn't forget the feeling of the chains of his magic around my throat, choking me, *binding me*, and draining my magic. I'd felt so weak and powerless.

What if he actually trapped me?

Matthias would have absolute power over me. He'd unleash me on the city and turn me against my friends. I'd become a monster like the djinn. What if I killed Rhiannon or Damian? That was what was at stake. Not my freedom. Not my sanity. Not revenge. But my friends and my home.

I felt sick.

Damian took my hand. "Look, the truth is, I don't have the magic to close the portal. And I can't go toe-to-toe with a genie if it attacks. I've got fire magic, but I'm not an efreet. You're the only one of us with that kind of power. Not me, not the angels, not the arch-mages. *You.*"

I let go of his hand and leaned against the railing, putting my palms against my head.

He was right. And the portal was everything. Matthias might slip away, but if we didn't get that portal shut...

"This is your call on how to proceed," he continued. "We can all go and make a stand at the gateway, or we can split up and I can distract Matthias while you shut the portal."

I rested my head against the post and weighed the options.

Closing the portal had to be our priority, and Ethan couldn't do it without my magic. I hadn't told Damian, but I was worried it would take a wish. He wouldn't want to risk the inevitable consequences, but it might be the only way.

As much as I wanted revenge against Matthias, Damian could buy us time to get it shut.

I didn't like the way my thoughts were leaning, and I let out sigh. "You know, whenever people split up in horror movies, they die."

He smiled. "Fair point. But I have no intention of that. I'm just trying to give us a fighting chance. Matthias distracted us with the attack on the Archives before he hit Bentham. We could do the same to him."

"I can't believe I'm considering this lunacy."

"We don't have to."

Memories of our past battles with Matthias tugged at my mind. "No. I think it could work. But won't Matthias just teleport away if you get the upper hand? He disappeared when I tried to pull him into the Realm of Water and vanished after Spark attacked him outside of Bentham."

"Teleporting and planes-walking are not part of his magic, as far as I know. He must be using some kind of transport charm. If we can surprise him, we can disarm him and knock it away. My hope is he'll hesitate for a single, fatal second when he sees me. We were allies for centuries, and I think he's still holding out some hope that he can turn me to his side."

"And you won't hesitate for exactly the same reasons?"

Damian brushed the hair away from my face. "I have a very good reason not to."

Warmth flooded me.

Planting my hands on his chest, I slowly pushed him back against the railing and dragged his mouth to mine. I'd give him a reminder of all the good reasons he had.

Gods, we'd better make it through this.

Two hours later, our team had assembled in an empty warehouse that Damian owned. Matthias seemed to have informants everywhere, so we had to keep a low profile.

Ethan had inscribed a large teleportation circle in the middle of the room—our gateway to the Realm of Chaos, aka Matthias's realm. It was based on the photographs Damian had taken during his visit to the Searing Citadel a week ago.

We hadn't activated the portal yet, but none of us stepped across the boundary. Teleportation circles could be touchy things, and no one wanted to accidently scuff a rune and send us all to Timbuktu.

The team was small. Jaxson and eight shifters. Nathaniel and a dozen other angels. Ethan, Rhiannon, and Spark. It wasn't much, but we needed stealth and speed more than we needed numbers, and most of the Order's personnel were busy preparing the city for attack. The rest of the angels would be ready to protect the city, too, if we failed.

I caught everyone's attention with a gust of wind. "As you all know, Matthias is assembling an army and is probably intending to invade Magic Side. We need to strike first and cripple their operation. Our objectives are to capture Matthias, close the gateway to the hells, and recover prisoners. Closing the gateway will be our number one priority. If we can't get it shut, I have no doubt that the city will be overwhelmed."

I passed out a series of sketches that Damian and I had made. "These are maps of the Searing Citadel, Matthias's base of operations in the Realm of Chaos. Damian and I are the only ones who've been in the tower before, so we'll each lead a team."

I gestured to Ethan, Rhiannon, and the assembled angels. "Our team is going to shut down the gateway to hell. Things are going to get rough. Ethan and I will unbind the spells keeping the gateway open. We don't know how long it will take, but if the portal is large, it might take time. Undoubtably, we'll be attacked from all sides—both by hordes of demons coming through the portal, as well as those already in Matthias's domain. The angels will keep the demons off, and when the genies show up, I'll keep them at bay."

Damian stepped forward. "Shifters, you're with me. We need to buy Neve time. We'll infiltrate the tower and ambush Matthias. Once he's neutralized, we'll free the prisoners and get them back to the portal. Stealth will be key. We need to preserve the element of surprise if we're going to have any shot at him."

I nodded. "We'll give Damian's team a five-minute head start to get to Matthias. Then we go."

"Where's the portal located? I don't see it on this map," Nathaniel asked.

"That's the tricky part. Matthias's fortress is positioned on an island of ice floating in midair. Our informant, Zara, told us that the gateway's not inside the tower. So, it's either right next to the tower or on an adjacent island of ice. We'll have to hunt for it, but it should be big. That means Ethan and Rhiannon, you're gonna have to hitch a ride with an angel to get there."

Rhiannon raised an eyebrow and gave Nathaniel a lascivious look. To be fair, he was unbelievably perfect if you liked pretty boys. She did.

Damian heaved a bag onto the table. "This mission is incredibly dangerous. We think we'll get the drop on Matthias, but things could go bad, fast. These are transport charms. If you're overrun, use them. If you get cornered, use them. No last stands. If this doesn't work, we'll need all of you to defend Magic Side, and we don't want to add to their cadre of captives."

I tossed a transport charm to Rhiannon and started passing out the rest to the shifters. "Any questions?"

22

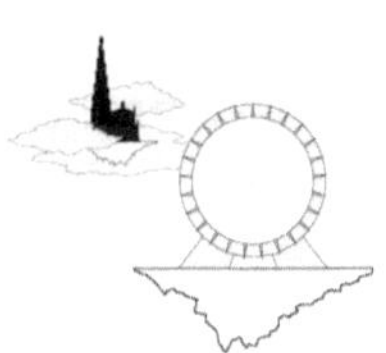

Damian

Jaxson and his shifters formed up around me at the edge of the teleportation circle. They were wearing tactical vests and armed with savage-looking knives.

I tapped a composite dagger on my belt. "Make sure you've got nothing metal on you. Matthias is an iron mage," I reminded them. "He'll use it against you."

"We got the memo. We've got fiberglass knives. No guns," Jaxson growled.

His expression was laser focused, and I could feel the restrained power of his aura, tightly coiled, like a viper, ready to strike.

"Remember, the angels want us to bring Matthias in alive. He'll have some sort of transport charm, and we'll need to stop him from using it. And Jaxson, if for a second you think he's going to get away, kill him. We can't risk him getting to Neve."

"Sounds like we should just kill him then." He gestured to Nathaniel at the edge of the room. "Fuck the angels."

My stomach twisted. Matthias had been my brother. And I'd be left with promises broken to Zara, Neve, and Nathaniel.

I nodded in assent and pulled my dagger from my belt. "Let's go."

Ethan and Neve lit up the teleportation circle. The runes around the edges sparked to life, and the circle burst into flames. The center started to undulate like a mirage, and we shot through.

The ether pulsed around me and shot into a dark chamber supported by tall, thin pillars.

A pair of demon sentries jerked to life as soon as we stepped through. I surged forward before they had a chance to react, ramming my knife through the neck of the one on the right as it started to shout out a warning. I tossed the body to the ground and spun.

The second demon lay on the floor beside Jaxson, its body broken and contorted in impossible ways. What had he done to it?

I reached for Matthias with my dragon sense. He was here. Close. Two floors down.

The runes of the teleportation ring crackled and sizzled with magic as the rest of the team burst through the portal one by one. I grabbed Neve's arm as she came through. "Only two sentries. Either Matthias has no idea we're coming, or this is a trap. Be on guard."

Neve grimaced. "I'll assume the worst."

"Who knows. Maybe we'll get lucky this time. Give me five minutes before you attack the gateway. By then, we'll have either brought Matthias down or created a big enough distraction to give you cover."

"Please be careful, Damian," she whispered.

I softly traced the line of her jaw, trying not to show how much I feared for her. "I will. You, too. Don't take any chances. If it looks like Matthias is going to corner you, planes-walk away. Let the angels handle him. The city needs you on its side."

She caught my wrist as I turned. "I need you at my side. Don't forget that."

I hadn't told her that I'd given up my angel powers.

"I won't forget." I turned and strode toward the door, my dragon roaring with each step.

Jaxson and his team were waiting at the exit. "All clear," he growled.

I listened at the doorway, even though Jaxson's senses were far superior to mine. He nodded and we slipped into the hall. The shifters all either had claws or knives out. It was time for close, quiet work.

Jaxson and I alternated the lead, leapfrogging each other from corridor to corridor. Some of the doorways led to barracks or guard rooms, and I quickly locked those with spells. Ultimately, our cover would be blown, and I wanted to slow their counterstrike as much as possible.

Matthias wasn't moving. That meant time was on our side.

Jaxson ducked his head around a corner, pulled back, and raised a hand. We stopped.

He held up three fingers. *Three demons.* Then he pointed at the two female shifters. They followed him around the corner with blinding speed. There was the muffled sound of combat, and then almost immediately, deathly silence.

I brought the rest of the team forward. Blue blood spattered the walls and dripped from Jaxson's clawed hands. I assumed all three demons were dead. Possibly more. It was difficult to tell from the carnage.

Even though the bodies would dissipate into smoke, remnants of the fight would be visible. Our clock was officially ticking.

One of the women had shifted into a wolf. She sniffed a disarticulated arm and then padded down the hall after Jaxson.

We slipped into the stairwell and raced two floors down, slitting three more demons' throats on the way. The wolves moved like ghosts, sticking to the shadows. I paused beside Jaxson at the next corridor and whispered. "We're close. Next room."

Matthias's presence felt like flames in my chest. Very close.

Jaxson nodded and held up four fingers. More than I would like. He could hear the heartbeats or smell them. Odds were, with four someone would make noise.

I motioned at three more werewolves. They stepped forward, and I drew a line across my throat. Slowly, I laid one hand into the other and mouthed, *Put them down quietly.*

The werewolves nodded and whipped around the corner. I jumped out and shot a bolt of ice through one demon's eyes and another bolt into the throat of a second. Two shifters caught and silenced both of mine, while Jaxson and the she-wolf ripped out the throats of the other two demons.

There had been one short exclamation. That was it.

I crept toward the door. Matthias was inside talking to someone. He wasn't alone. Jaxson cocked his head for a second and held up two fingers. *Good.*

I quickly wove a spell to unlock the door, then I turned and nodded to the shifters. We burst in.

Matthias looked up in shock as I slung a bolt of ice straight into his chest. It was a glorious moment.

I surged into the room as a purple demon roared, leapt over the desk, and unleashed a cloud of balefire. Necrotic burns blistered across my exposed skin, though my efreeti magic protected me from the worst of the flames. I unleashed a storm of hail, but the purple flames swirling around the demon melted it instantly.

Guess I'm fighting fire with fire.

Matthias staggered to his feet and reached for a beaded necklace around his neck. A transport charm.

As if reading my mind, Jaxson and his wolves tore into the room. Jaxson rebounded off the wall and slammed into Matthias. He ripped the transport charm from Matthias's neck, leaving a set of bloody claw marks in his wake.

I ducked the demon's massive fist as Matthias drove a gleaming dagger into Jaxson's shoulder. Before I could shout a warning, Matthias flicked his wrist and Jaxson hurtled through the air.

Power over metal.

I blasted a bolt of fire into the demon's face, and two wolves grabbed his arms. I whipped my dagger out and finished him with one deft thrust through the base of his skull.

Jaxson yanked the dagger from his shoulder, flicked it through the barred window, and gave a savage growl.

I pointed my bloody knife at Matthias. "It's over, old friend. Submit."

He arched his eyebrows. "Oh, I'm certain we can come to some arrangement. How about I pay you off?"

Matthias flicked his hand and a chest on the desk exploded. Coins sprayed through the room like a shotgun blast.

I flung up a thin wall of ice just in time, but Jaxson and his wolves took the brunt of the shrapnel. Howls erupted throughout the room as coins and ice chips rained down around me. Gold, thank fates. Silver would have wiped out the wolves. Even so, those in the room were tattered and bloody.

Matthias shouted and darted into the adjacent room. Before I could follow, a roar shook the corridor behind me. I spun as a tsunami of water surged down the hall, sweeping a couple wolves away.

Water poured into the room and knocked me off my feet. I grabbed the edge of the desk and hauled myself up. Where was Jaxson?

The marid loomed in the doorway, a devilish grin on his face.

Gods damn it.

We'd been so close, and now Matthias was gone, and I had to deal with this asshole. Rage shook my body, and I thrust my hands out, freezing the marid's legs into a solid block of ice.

His smile vanished, and grim satisfaction took me as I pushed my magic forward, freezing the very water in his veins and wrapping him in a column of ice. He screamed in anger and pain.

Jaxson burst up from the water and staggered forward, still in human form. He slashed his claws through the ice and into the marid's chest.

"We don't like getting wet," he snarled.

The marid's eyes burned with fear, and with a puff of steam, he vanished.

Damned planes-walkers.

"You've got to be shitting me," Jaxson growled.

The werewolf turned. The blast of coins had ripped his face and arms, though the tactical vest protected most of his body. He'd heal soon with his shifter blood. "Where's that fucker, Matthias? I've got his transportation necklace, so he can't have gone far."

I pointed to the adjacent room. "Ran like a coward. Let's take him down."

Even though I'd lost my knife in the churn, I didn't dare draw my sword or spear. Matthias could turn them back against me. He'd done it before.

I snapped my hand and formed an ice knife. The perfect thing to ram through his heart. Neve had made a blood oath with Zara, not me, and if it came down to him or her, I'd kill him in an instant.

As soon as I looked around the doorway, an explosion rocked the tower. I dodged back as rubble rained down around us. The water swirled around my legs, and the current picked up.

Bad sign.

Ducking around the corner, I shot a barrage of hail to cover my advance. But Matthias was gone, and there was a gaping hole where a window had once been. Water cascaded out of the gap, with only purple-blue sky beyond.

I cursed and dashed to the hole, struggling to keep my balance in the outflow. Bracing myself against the wall, I looked out.

A bolt of agony shot through me, and I glanced down at the iron spear rammed into my chest. I caught myself against the stonework as the water threatened to drop me over the edge. I'd given up my wings, and it was a long way down.

I sucked in a breath, and my lungs rasped as pain spiked through my body. There'd be no healing this time.

"He's out there," I growled to Jaxson, grabbing the spear to pull it free. As soon as I tugged, the iron spear drove deeper into my chest, as if it had a mind of its own —Matthias's magic. The point erupted out of my back. "I may need some help getting this out."

Suddenly, the spear bent back on itself, and dug into my back like a fishhook. My body jerked forward, driving the air from my lungs. Jaxson grabbed for my arm, but Matthias's magic yanked me through the open window and into the sky beyond.

But my angel powers were gone. I couldn't fly. I couldn't heal.

All I could do was watch the obsidian tower recede into the distance as I plummeted down into the infinite space below.

23

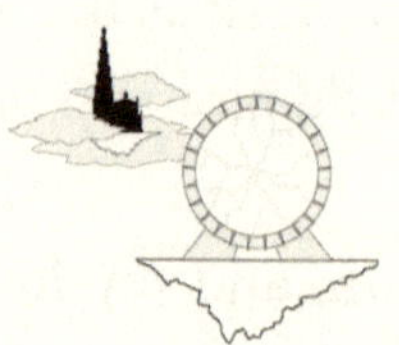

Neve

My clunky plastic wristwatch counted the minutes.

It wasn't stylish, but we'd had to leave anything metal behind, just in case Matthias tried to turn them against us. That included cell phones, watches, daggers, and belts.

Luckily, I could dismiss the khanjar Damian had made me whenever I needed to, so I could still do some knife work if it came to that.

I touched the opal necklace Rhiannon had given me so long ago for good luck. It had been with me this long, through the djinn's maze and the efreet's fortress, so clearly it had some good mojo working for it. I'd even restrung the opal on a silk chain, so Matthias couldn't choke me with it. I hated doing that, but I couldn't part with it entirely.

Rhiannon scuffed her foot impatiently. She wasn't too happy about leaving her swords behind, but she still had her intelligent bolas named Herc, a composite knife, and even a tonfa—a type of baton with a side handle.

The angels had glowing swords. Either they were magic and not affected by Matthias's power, or they didn't care. I wasn't going to grill them about it. Every muscle in my body was on alert, and my stomach felt like I'd just chugged a pitcher of curdled milk. I forced myself to breathe. This was it.

Rhiannon grabbed my hand. Normally, she would have been gabbing to put me at ease, but we had to be quiet. She nodded her head at the angels and mouthed, *They're so hot.*

I suspected Rhia was going to have trouble going back to normal guys after seeing the angels in battle. I rolled my eyes and responded, *All yours. P.S. They're kinda jerks.*

Nathaniel was beautiful, but cold. Unreadable, unapproachable, and well, an ass, as far as I was concerned. Damian had never been like that, had he? There was always a fire burning behind his green eyes.

I wished he were here with me. I hated splitting up, but if we could simultaneously knock out Matthias and the portal, we'd neutralize the threat to Magic Side in one fell swoop. It might be our only shot.

Spark scampered over to me, though scampered

might not have been an appropriate word for a twelve-foot-long dragon. *Are there snacks?*

"Plenty of demons to munch on," I whispered.

Disappointing. Their essence is bad and not tasty.

"What's really on your mind?" I could tell that he wasn't really interested in food.

You are nervous. I am trying to put you at ease.

"Thanks, Spark, but I don't think that's going to happen. I'm just going over things in my mind."

Ethan had taught me the incantation to break the spell keeping the gateway open. I'd memorized it quickly, which was a gift, but I had to be sure I got it right. I kept going over it, line by line.

Finally, my watch beeped. "Okay. Go time."

My team formed up behind me, and Spark turned into a little mote of light to guide our way.

We darted left out of the chamber. The angels were silent like ghosts, making my own footsteps seem deafening in the empty corridors. I recalled Nathaniel's monstrous footsteps when we'd met in Armenia. Bastard must have been showing off because he was as silent as a mouse now.

Heart pounding, I stopped at each intersection, checking the way. Two hallways down, we turned right.

A couple of demons leaned against the wall, guarding a door. Before they could cry out, I squeezed my fists and sucked the breath from their lungs using my power over air. *Practice for Matthias*, I thought, smiling. Though his innate resistance to my magic would be far stronger than these two.

The demons clutched their throats and fell to their knees. The angels were on them in a second, finishing the job with glowing blades. The demons' bodies slumped onto the stone and began evaporating into trails of smoke.

They would be reborn in the underworld. I hoped that process took a very long time, because there was an open gateway to the hells just outside the tower, and I didn't want anyone we'd killed coming back for vengeance.

We ducked into a stairwell and raced up four floors until we reached a padlocked iron door leading to one of the citadel's many balconies.

I pointed at the locked door. "This one."

One of the angels cut through the lock with a single swipe and shoved the door open. Extending beyond the balcony was a mesmerizing realm I'd only seen through Damian's memories. It was far stranger in person.

The sky was like a nebula—a boiling thunderstorm of strangely colored clouds that bathed everything in a purple light. Islands of ice floated through the sky. It seemed that Matthias hadn't captured an earth genie yet, because there was no stone or earth in this artificial world.

In many ways, it reminded me of Mavia's frosty domain in the Realm of Air, but the magic was all wrong. The signature of the place was maddening, like a thousand people whispering different things in your ears all at once.

And in the center of it all was the hellgate.

The massive iron ring stood erect in the middle of a floating island of ice. The center of the ring was filled with liquid flame that undulated like waves. Streams of magic poured out of the gateway, dissipating in the sky above.

"Damn," Ethan whispered, at my side. "It's bigger than I thought. That's going to take some time to disable."

There were a few demons guarding the ring—hulking yellow monsters with broad wings. Every few seconds, another demon or two would fly in or out of the portal on some errand.

I turned back to my team. "That portal leads straight to one of the hells. Once we strike, our first priority is to make sure no demons get through to alert whatever is lurking on the other side."

I pointed to the two angels we'd assigned to keep the gateway clear. "Rhiannon can stop time for a few seconds. That should give you time if things get out of hand and you're overwhelmed. The rest of you will defend Ethan as he unbinds the spells powering it. We'll need to hit hard and fast. I'll make a beachhead. Everyone, follow as fast as you can."

Rhiannon squeezed my shoulder, and I gripped her

hand. My heart was pounding so hard, I could barely hear myself think.

This was it. No turning back.

Stepping onto the balcony, I exploded through the sky like a bullet. I was at the gateway in seconds.

Matthias wasn't here, so I whipped out my khanjar and ripped into one of the demons guarding the portal. He screeched in anger, but I put him down in two strokes.

His buddy leapt for the gateway, but Spark shifted into a dragon and dropped him to the ground. I knocked a third demon down with a blast and summoned a whirling vortex of air in front of the portal to trap anyone trying to get through.

The demon scrambled back to his feet and lashed out at me with his clawed hand. I jumped back, but his reach was longer than I expected. His claws ripped into my left shoulder, and pain flared through my arm.

He was about four times my size, but I could use that to my advantage. I spun inside his reach, ducked low, and slammed my blade into his knee. I juiced it with a burst of wind and knocked him face down onto the ice.

Leaping on his back, I finished him with three fast stabs while Spark ripped the head off his demon and looked around for more.

Angels alighted on the icy island, and I released a vortex of air around us so Ethan and I could get to work.

There were glowing runes inscribed around the ring

—just like a teleportation circle. Ethan pointed, and shouted over the wind, "We'll have to disable each rune, one at a time!"

We began casting the disenchantment spells, and our magic crackled along the ring. The runes around the edge of the portal sparked and flickered, and finally two faded out.

The ring shook and groaned like a suspension bridge twisting in a storm, but the fiery portal at its center remained.

Ethan broke off his spellcraft. "This thing is possessed by some serious magic. It's going to take time, and I'm betting they know we're here by now. Get ready!"

I glanced back at the citadel. It was unsettling to see the jet-black tower floating on an island in the middle of the sky rather than where it belonged—in the midst of a lava lake.

Everything about this place was wrong and disjointed, like a patchwork of images cut out of random magazines. A work in progress, I gathered.

The realm was clearly unstable, which was why Matthias had needed so much magic to hold it together. Even the obsidian tower seemed on shaky footing. It listed slightly to one side, and dozens of chains anchored it to the ice island, straining to hold it upright.

Maybe there was a way we could use that.

As I looked on, the door to the balconies flew open

and dozens of demons soared out. Unfortunately, the tower was only seven or eight hundred feet away, so they'd be on us soon.

"Here they come!" I shouted over my shoulder as I disabled another rune. As I broke the spell, it released foul magic that made my stomach churn.

Rhiannon rushed to defend the portal, while Nathaniel and two angels joined me at my side.

"Ready?" I asked.

Nathaniel gave me an impenetrable look as his sword flared with light. His magic washed over me unabated. Pomegranates and dates. The sound of bells and wind rushing through abandoned canyons. His power felt ancient, like crumbling ruins. How many civilizations had he watched rise and fall? "We've been fighting demons for thousands of years. So, yes, child. We're ready."

I grinned. "Good. I'll let you pick off the stragglers then."

I summoned a roiling wall of wind. The descending demons spun in the storm, crashing into each other, wings snapping. I twisted the currents with my hands and slammed disoriented monsters into the icy isle before turning my attention back to the portal.

"Stragglers, it is." Nathaniel smirked and launched into the air on pearl-white wings.

Winged demons in more varieties than I'd ever seen divebombed us from all directions. They screeched and howled in their unnatural tongue as they lashed out with razor-sharp talons and jagged swords.

The angels set to dismembering them with their glowing blades. Nathaniel was impossibly fast. I could barely track his movements out of the corner of my eyes, and I was relieved to have him watching my back. He decapitated one demon with a single stroke, spun and rammed his blade through another. While Damian was a raging firestorm, Nathaniel was cold grace.

For all Nathaniel's ability, I wished I had that firestorm beside me now.

Screeching and sounds of chaos erupted as a flood of hideous, jabbering demons skittered out of the gateway. Six arms sprouted from their iridescent bodies, and they moved like insects, running on their arms like spiders and then suddenly springing through the air.

"What the hell are those?" I screamed as I dropped my spell and blasted one out of the sky with a gust of wind.

It landed on its back, tumbled over, and struck out with four of its hands. Claws dug into my side, and I screamed in anger, flipping it into the air before ramming my dagger into its skull. The iridescent blood coating my hand evaporated in smoke.

Looking up, I counted a dozen monsters swarming around Ethan. *Crap.* They were clearly aware of what we were doing. Nathaniel appeared at his side in an instant, sweeping his blade in an arc like a reaper cutting wheat.

A ring of demon corpses piled up around them, and smoke rose from the bodies as they disintegrated, creating a wall of thick haze.

Dread filled me. This was a hopeless task. As soon as one demon dropped, more clambered out of the gateway. They climbed along the sides of the ring and leapt down, screaming. I could knock them away with blasts of wind, but it meant I was making no progress on disabling the portal.

Rhiannon turned to the angels at her side. "We're getting overrun! Ready to even the odds?"

In answer, they dismissed their swords and pulled bows from the ether.

"Now!" she screamed.

Time around the gateway slowed to a crawl. Demons were caught half in and half out of the ring, while others floated midair, suspended midleap.

The angels released a barrage of arrows, and the air filled with blinding flashes of light as they found their marks and exploded.

After a few seconds, time resumed.

Disarticulated demon chunks splattered around us, and a wave of nausea worked its way through me.

Rhiannon staggered back, weak from the effort. "Get ready to go again!"

Shrieks sounded behind me, and I tore my gaze away from the gateway and blasted two more demons out of the sky. They'd be back quick.

Angels soared around me, cutting down demon after demon. My heart wrenched as one of the glowing beings disappeared over the edge, entangled by demons.

Rhiannon shouted, and a series of flashes followed. Seconds later, more demon bits plummeted down around me.

I leapt into the air and cut one down as it dove toward Rhia. We crashed into the ice, and the demon's claws raked at me, but I blasted him back, and then ripped my dagger through his throat.

"Thanks!" Rhia hollered back.

I was about to respond when the wind around us rose. My breath caught as the taste of tobacco burned my tongue and the scent of frankincense filled the air. I met Rhia's wide eyes. We both knew that signature all too well.

A sudden windstorm ripped across the ice and knocked me off my feet. Iridescent demons spiraled through the sky, arms and legs flailing. Cruel laughter echoed around us like rolling thunder.

The djinn had arrived.

And with him, a hurricane.

24

Damian

Wind whipped past as I plummeted down. The obsidian tower on its floating island of ice was rapidly becoming a speck.

Rage shook through me. I was helpless without wings. The *arrogance* of angels.

I shoved down the pain and rage. I had to think clearly, fast. How was I going to get back into the fight?

My only option was to planes-walk or use a transport charm. I would probably survive the leap through the cosmos, but I wouldn't be able to get back to the Realm of Chaos without—

Agony ripped through my body, and the wind rushed out of my lungs.

I was no longer falling. There was only pain. I tried

to move but choked on blood. Mounds of white danced before my eyes, and my vision faded in and out.

Somewhere beyond the pain, the ground was cold. I moved a single finger. Soft snow. Ice.

I must have struck a floating iceberg or island. A fall like that would have killed a normal man, so my stolen powers must have kept me alive. I glanced down at the massive iron spear lodged in my chest. My healing magic was gone, which meant that I was a dead man.

I drew a little of the efreet's fire to warm my body. Pain trickled through me with the effort, and I knew I wouldn't survive planes-walking or transporting out of there. I wouldn't be seeing Neve again.

Fire shot through my chest, and the dragon within me screamed in agony.

Of all the things, why had they taken my angelic magic?

The clouds churned in the sky above. My foggy mind drifted. Different clouds appeared, clouds from a day centuries ago. I was either hallucinating or dead.

Ancient memories overtook my mind as I drifted out of consciousness. I was no longer lying on this gods-forsaken chunk of ice, but bleeding in the hard dirt, the last fragments of my soul barely clinging to my mortal body. My enemies lay strewn around me. Carnage. A massacre. I'd fought like a madman, but in the end, they'd brought me down.

I turned my head and choked as blood seeped from

the corners of my mouth. My city still stood. That was all that mattered. They had hated me here, ostracized me for being a FireSoul. But in the end, I'd been able to save them. Save the kind few, amongst the bad.

It was a worthy death.

"You must decide," a voice boomed overhead. Though this was just a memory, it was as clear as the day it had happened.

My head rolled back to the heavens. The radiant angel loomed over me, pestering me with his questions.

Would he not let me die in peace? Bring an end to my dark and corrupt life?

A second angel joined his side. "We have asked you for the last time. Either rise and join our ranks as one of the angels or release your mortal coil and depart for the netherworld. You must choose."

I tried to speak, but the only sound was a rasping gurgle.

The first angel knelt. "You are a brave warrior and strong of spirit to fight your inner dragon for so long. The path of the angels is not kind, one of arduous toil and heartbreak. If you are not strong enough to watch the world tear itself apart, then you should pass on to the next world. The choice is yours."

They were too radiant to look at, and I had to avert my eyes.

"Let us leave him, Nathaniel," the second angel said.

"Choose," the angel commanded.

The dragon in my soul screamed with fury. This didn't have to be the end. There was something more it needed, that it craved, and I hadn't yet found it.

So be it.

Pain wracked my body as I rolled to my front, slumping face first in the bloody soil. I shoved myself upward but collapsed to my knees. My chest heaved as I rammed my blade into the barren soil and pushed myself up, standing straight and proud before the assembled angels.

"Choose." Nathaniel's word echoed across time like he was standing before me now.

I had chosen life on that day, long ago. That last spark of my soul had dragged me to my feet, and I had become a being of light. An angel.

Choose. Nathaniel's voice resounded in my mind.

It had been a choice. The Watchers had done nothing to make me an angel. *I* had made myself.

A desperate hope tugged at me.

Could they have truly taken my angelic power away?

The djinn had laughed when I'd wished to no longer be a FireSoul. He'd said that no magic in heaven or on earth could change what I was—and I was an angel, as much as I was a FireSoul.

I hadn't given up on that dusty battlefield all those years ago, and I wouldn't give up now. Neve was up there, somewhere in the sky. The only person who mattered. The thing my dragon had craved for centuries on end. And she was fighting for her life.

Agony lanced my soul. I wouldn't let her down. I would protect. I would defend. I had risen once before, and I would do it again.

Rolling onto my side, I growled as I shoved myself to my knees, rejecting failure. Rejecting death.

And with that act of defiance, my angelic powers awoke.

Magic roared through me, fire in my veins. My bones snapped together, and my wounds shut with bursts of flame. I shoved the spear through my body and out my back, wincing as my flesh knit itself together.

I was an angel, reborn. I looked to the sky. Neve was up there. Her spirit called to me, pulling on my soul. A high-tension cable. A chain that could never be broken.

I searched for Matthias with my dragon sense. He was far from her—but closing in impossibly fast.

Anger poured through me like wildfire—flames of an unquenchable thirst. I would protect her, no matter the cost.

Power surged through me, and I roared at the heavens as pain wracked my body and a pair of burning wings ripped free from my back.

I was no longer an angel of light or dark, but of fire and vengeance.

And my vengeance would not be denied. I leapt into the sky.

Neve

The hurricane tightened around us like a noose.

The wind screamed in my ears and ripped chunks of ice from the ground. Shattered fragments spun around us like a cloud of daggers.

Neither angel nor demon could fly.

Rhiannon screamed as she slipped and slid across the ice, but Nathaniel was at her side in a second. He rammed his blade into the ground as an anchor and summoned a golden shield from the ether, raising it over their heads to block the deadly onslaught of ice shards.

Ethan dropped down beside them, and more angels landed nearby. Anchoring themselves with their blades, they raised their shields to create a glinting wall of gold in the face of the storm.

Splinters of ice whipped toward me like spears, but I deflected them with an explosion of wind.

An angel ran for me, but I shook my head. I wouldn't cower before the djinn. I could hear his laughter in the thunder. His hubris. He sickened me, and I wouldn't let him take what was mine.

And the sky was mine. The wind was mine.

I spoke the name of the storm and felt power surge through my veins. Then with a gust, my body was no more. I was a cyclone amidst the hurricane.

I poured my anger into the wind. The djinn's magic spun around me, so I spun the other way, grinding against his power like a wheel against a blade. I would grind him into nothing.

My power swelled and pushed outward, creating a calm around my allies. I pushed harder as the djinn shoved back, and the island shook and shattered as we battered against each other.

The djinn howled and released a barrage of lightning bolts through the sky, but they meant nothing to me. I was a storm. The only thing that mattered was which of us was stronger and would remain.

I had no mercy for him. Damian had given him his freedom once, and he'd used it to rampage. He'd abducted Rhiannon. And now he served Matthias with a hatred for all beings.

He had a truly twisted heart. And I would tear it apart.

Ethan shouted as demons flooded out of the gateway like a plague of rats. He hadn't been able to finish breaking the spell.

Nathaniel and the angels formed a wall, swinging their blades with deadly efficiency as demon corpses dropped to the ground below, smoke rising from their cuts and severed limbs. Time pulsed as Rhiannon slowed the monsters and aided the strikes of the angels, but I knew if I did nothing more, they'd soon be overrun.

Thunder cracked and ice exploded as the djinn launched bolts of lightning into the fray. One of the angels screamed and plunged from the sky—a haunting noise that I would never forget.

Rage consumed me. It was time to destroy. "Spark, I need your fire!"

I'm here.

The sprite appeared for a single moment, then disappeared as his magic flowed through me, like when we'd fought the hydra. We were one, and our magic was one.

I turned the winds to flame, and thunder boomed as a firestorm erupted around me. The flying chunks of ice burst into steam, and the island began to melt below. The conflagration roared and spread, feeding on the djinn's magic, devouring his power.

He screamed, and I felt the hurricane weaken. And then it ceased.

The djinn fled across the sky.

Spark's voice flickered in my mind like a sputtering candle. *Finish him. I've got a little juice left.*

I released the cyclone of fire, and the flames flickered into the sky. I became myself again and flew after the bastard who had begun it all, who'd captured my friend, and who'd tried to kill me again and again. But I'd defeated his windstorm, and I would defeat him. I was stronger.

Fueled by Spark's power, I shot through the air like a

flaming comet and slammed into the djinn with my dagger drawn. I poured the rest of Spark's magic through the blade as it sunk into him. He howled, and I felt Spark's presence vanish as he departed back to the Realm of Fire to recharge.

But it was enough.

Flames burst from the djinn's eyes, and he dissolved into a plume of black smoke.

I gasped. It was over.

My body shook as wave after wave of exhaustion overtook me. The gateway was far away, but I could see my friends battling for their lives against the demon horde.

My heart sank. One down, ten thousand to go.

I turned to go back, but a cold voice cut into my back like a knife. A spell of binding.

Matthias.

25

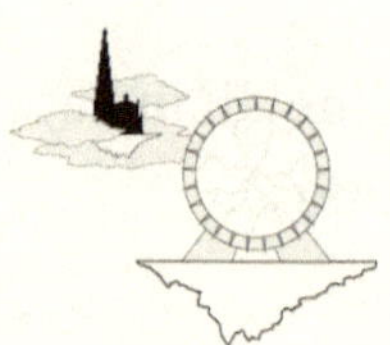

Neve

I spun.

Matthias dropped from the sky on the back of a black firedrake with burning wings.

Panic speared my heart as I dodged a jet of fire. I tried to planes-walk away, but the chains of his binding spell had already wrapped around me like a noose, anchoring me to this realm. Agonizing pain tore through my chest as the spell tightened like a vice grip. My ribs felt like they were going to crack like matchsticks.

I ducked away from the drake's massive talons and twisted underneath, shooting it with a blast of wind. But the creature was over a hundred feet long, my magic was practically useless, and I was beyond exhausted.

Anger shook my body. I wouldn't go this way. The sky was still *mine*.

Summoning all my reserves of power, I flew as fast as I could toward the tower. It was probably filled with a ton of demons, but the firedrake couldn't follow me in there, and it was my primary concern right now. As well as the bastard casting spells from its back, of course.

A burst of flame arced across my body, and I screamed as I rolled right. The drake was almost on me, and its jaws snapped inches from my head.

Fates be damned, was he trying to kill me or capture me?

Pain erupted through my legs as the creature's tail crashed into me. Both, it seemed.

I dove down to avoid another jet of fire, but for all my effort, I couldn't shake them. The words of Matthias's spell wrapped around me. It siphoned my magic and used the power to bind me, so the bonds grew stronger as I grew weaker.

I knew exactly how it worked—I'd used it to bind the djinn. And unfortunately, Matthias was far more experienced than I'd been.

I strained to get ahead, but the firedrake was too fast, and the invisible chains strengthened, link by link.

The monster's tail lashed at me again with its poisoned barb. I dodged but spun out of control. It was on me in a second. A massive claw closed around my waist, and I screamed as the wind burst from my lungs.

Fighting for consciousness, I summoned my khanjar

and sank it into the drake's massive claw again and again, but it was useless. I was a mosquito. The claws tightened as its searing blood poured over me. The bastard had me.

I blasted the enormous beast with wind to no avail.

Matthias hadn't stopped chanting. I could barely hear his voice above the roar of the wind, but I didn't need to hear the spell to know that it was working just as he'd planned.

A translucent collar formed around my throat, and horror flooded my veins. It was almost done. If only I had Spark's fire magic right now. I'd blow myself to smithereens if it meant escaping Matthias's bonds.

A black spear flew across my field of vision and rammed into the side of the drake. The beast roared as ice magic crackled over its scales.

Damian dropped out of the sky, an avenging angel with burning eyes and wings.

My gods. What in the fates had happened to Damian?

Joy cascaded through my heart, and then agony as the drake crushed me in its claws. I gasped in pain as several of my ribs cracked. *Gods make it end.*

Damian was a blur.

He soared through the air, and with one savage stroke of his burning blade, he sliced through the monster's foot. Black blood sprayed across me, scalding my flesh, but the claw released, and I plummeted through the sky.

The monster's screech ripped through the air behind me like shattering glass.

A burst of hail exploded from Damian's hands and blasted Matthias off the back of his mount.

Matthias howled in pain, and the spell broke.

Holy fates. I was free.

Rage surged through me like a churning river. Pulling my khanjar from the ether, I shot forward for the kill, but the drake wheeled and slammed its wing into me like a shield. I tried to scream but the pain from my ribs was too much, and I doubled over. The dagger flew from my hand and disappeared as I spun head over heels. This was not helping matters.

Gritting my teeth against the gods awful pain, I pulled out of the spin in time to see Damian dive for Matthias, ice spear raised for the kill.

Then the vicious barb of the drake's tail dug into his back and wrenched him into the sky. The enormous monster's head shot out and clamped down on Damian's legs.

Damian roared with a primal rage and rammed the spear into the monster's eye. Flames billowed from its mouth, but its grip on Damian didn't release as they plummeted downward through the sky.

Shock cascaded over me like a tidal wave.

"Planes-walk!" I screamed as I dove after them,

channeling my power to make my voice boom through the air.

I hated to leave, but it was our only choice. Closing my eyes, I drew on my bond with Spark and imagined the Realm of Fire because that's where Damian would be.

The cosmos spun around me, then my body jerked as Matthias's spell wrapped around me, pulling me back from the brink of escape.

My heart wrenched as I saw the drake spiraling down with Damian. *He hadn't planes-walked.*

And just like that, they disappeared.

I whirled around, clutching my throbbing ribs and reaching for the transport charm in my pocket.

Matthias hovered in the air ahead, a look of triumph on his face. With the flick of his hand, he tore the charm from my grasp and flung it through the air.

"You asshole!" I screamed, unleashing a jet of wind. He snapped his wings and easily darted away.

Smiling, he held up his enchanted bottle and beckoned with his hand.

I strained against his bonds and flew wildly though the air, but he followed easily. I could barely breathe from the broken ribs, and my magic was nearly exhausted.

"Spark! I need you now!" I cried.

Trying.

His voice was far away. He hadn't yet recovered his

magic. I choked back tears, desperately looking for a way out. My stomach churned. There was only one exit from this realm—the portal to hell.

Could I get through?

Matthias's spell tightened.

It was an insane plan, but it was my only chance to get away. Even if I couldn't, Rhiannon was there. The angels were there.

I hoped.

I could barely make out the magical gateway flickering on the far side of the tower. Ethan had almost broken the spell. I prayed it would hold a little longer and dove past the Searing Citadel.

Something heavy slammed into my side, and pain rocketed through my broken ribs. I dropped in an uncontrolled spiral and nausea overwhelmed me. Then my body jerked to a sudden halt as a cold iron chain wrapped around my leg.

Shit, no.

It was one of the chains that anchored the Searing Citadel to the floating island of ice. Before I could react, it yanked me back, reeling me in toward the tower, obeying Matthias's will.

I was a fish, hooked on a line.

I surged upward, my muscles straining to get away. The iron chain vibrated under the tension, and I groaned as I desperately tried to pull it free.

Matthias used his magic to wrench another anchor

chain from the ice. It shot upward and wrapped around my left leg. Then a third.

I struggled against the ice-cold iron, but the chains pulled me down toward the tower. Toward Matthias.

I looked wildly around for Damian, but he hadn't returned. I was so close to the portal. My friends were there. Nathaniel stood amidst a ring of smoking demon corpses. He fought like a man possessed, keeping them off Ethan. Rhiannon was at his side.

I screamed for help, but my words didn't carry. Overrun with demons, none of them looked up.

My body quaked with pain and anger. I wouldn't be bound.

Summoning the last of my strength, I called a bolt of lightning from the clouds, attacking the stone where the chains were anchored. Thunder cracked, and chunks of obsidian exploded outward. The chain broke free, but another leapt up to take its place.

Matthias didn't stop chanting his binding spell. With each word, my power drained away. Fatigue rolled over me, but I kept fighting. I couldn't hear his incantation, but I knew the words by heart. He'd taught them to me, and I'd used them to bind the djinn.

The irony consumed me as smoke trailed off my skin and downward into Matthias's bottle.

This was exactly what I'd done to the djinn.

The thing I'd feared most in the world, I'd done to

another of my kind. The djinn was a monster. A kidnapper. A destroyer. But after what I'd done to him, wasn't I?

Was this some kind of sick balance of fate?

I fought against the chains as desperation tore into me. "I wish that I couldn't be bound!"

Nothing happened. No magic sparked within me. Of course, it wouldn't—I couldn't grant myself wishes. Besides, I was too drained to grant one anyway.

But I had to try.

Matthias's spell vibrated through my body. Each word chipped away a piece of my freedom, a fragment of my soul.

In a blinding fury, I screamed the words back at Matthias, pouring bitterness and irony into each syllable, as if repeating them gave me any kind of power.

If this was how I was going to go, then I would be the one to say them, not some demon bastard.

My throat caught as an idea burst to light.

Matthias had taught me how to bind a djinn. Once bound to an object, a genie couldn't be bound to another. Frantic hope surged through me.

What if I cast the spell first?

On myself. I had no idea what would happen, but Matthias wouldn't be able to bind me if I was already bound.

But bound to myself? Would that work, or was it sheer madness?

The iron chains pulled me down to within twenty

feet of Matthias. This was it. Madness didn't matter anymore.

I knew the incantation by heart, but the spell also required a powerful object and something precious. Matthias had an enchanted bottle and my old khanjar.

I summoned the khanjar Damian had made for me —a powerful object that I could keep safe in the ether. I ripped Rhiannon's necklace from my neck—the most precious thing I owned.

My throat suddenly tightened as a phantom collar formed around my neck and translucent cuffs wrapped around my wrists. It was almost over.

Triumph shone in Matthias eyes.

This madness was my only shot. I stopped fighting against the iron chains and poured all my exhausted anger and terror into resisting his binding spell. Pressing the opal against my dagger, I shouted the words of the incantation I knew so well.

My voice boomed like thunder, but I didn't recognize any of the words I said. I didn't speak the incantation as Matthias had taught me.

I spoke the language of the djinn, the song of creation—the unwritten language that had once divided day from night, that had once divided the sky and the land and the sea.

The unearthly words hung like sunlight in the air.

I'd spoken the language only twice before—when I'd healed Damian and when I'd banished the marid, but it was part of my soul. It was the language of magic and life and possibility.

My tongue wove the complex incantation into five simple words that had been true since the dawn of time.

"I am my own master."

26

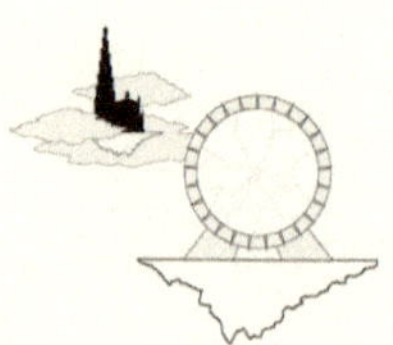

Neve

Time stilled.

Not even the sky breathed.

Then the universe exploded outward. I gasped as the vast power of the cosmos ripped through me. My tattoos flared like dying stars, and my body shook with magic.

My binding spell wrapped around me and my khanjar, an impregnable armor against Matthias. *Against anyone* who would ever try to dominate me. A truth so powerful that no one could ever take it from me.

The bonds of Matthias's spell shattered as if they were nothing.

Possibilities rose and fell around me like waves on the ocean. Never had I felt so alive. So free. So limitless.

I touched the chains around my legs, and they crumbled to rust—nothing more than red dust filtering down from the sky.

Light poured from my eyes as I saw the world for what it was. All the possibilities of reality.

And I turned on Matthias. "You."

His useless, pathetic incantation died on his lips.

Fury surged through my body, so much that I could no longer contain it. The clouds around me billowed into thunderheads, dark and ominous. Lightning leapt from my skin.

Matthias saw my true form and fled. But the sky was mine to command.

I snapped my fingers, and the thunderhead formed into a massive arm, mine to control. I reached out with it and snatched Matthias from the sky.

He writhed in the grip of the clouds, and I felt him struggling in the palm of my hand as if he were there, gripped like a doll. If I closed my fist, I would crush him like a bug. He was nothing compared to my power. My voice boomed like thunder. "You are mine."

The skies quaked and lightning burst around him, and Matthias screamed in horror. I pressed my thumb against his chest, and he gasped, his scream stifled.

A torrent of rage, power, and elation surged through my veins.

"Mercy!" he cried.

Anger consumed me, and lightning lashed out with each of my words. "Three times you tried to bind me.

You gave me over to the efreet to be tortured, to be a plaything. You unleashed the genies on Magic Side, and you were going to tear the city down with an army of demons. You deserve no mercy."

"I was trying to create a new world for our kind!"

I squeezed the breath from his lungs so I wouldn't have to listen to his words anymore. "Look around, Matthias. You've created nothing but chaos and destruction!"

I could end it all. That was justice. Pleasure poured through me as I started to squeeze the clouds tighter around him.

Then a new emotion rolled across my skin. A pleasure so pure that vengeance was like dust in my mouth. It came with the scent of ancient forests, the sound of crashing waves, and a whiskey voice that was so smooth it felt like silk wrapped around me. "Neve."

He was here.

Damian rose before me on flaming wings.

"Damian." My voice broke, no longer a thunderclap. No longer stronger than a breeze. "You're alive."

He grinned. "It was only a small dragon. No match for mine—and I wanted to be back with you, more than anything in the world."

Radiant warmth flowed through me. But there was time for this later. I looked back at Matthias. "I have him."

"I knew you would. Now it's time to deliver him to the angels."

The world reeled around me.

We'd actually won.

The gateway below had crumbled, and the remaining demons had fled. Matthias was alone, as I had been moments before.

One quick squeeze, and he would never hurt anyone again. He didn't deserve justice or mercy. He had blood on his hands.

But if I did this, so would I. Could I live with that?

I'd made a blood oath to Zara. I'd cut my hand and bound it to hers. She had given up her father for the promise that he wouldn't be killed.

I didn't care about the blood oath. Nothing in this world could bind me anymore, not Matthias's spell or demon magic. But I'd spent my life longing for my parents, and I wouldn't do the same to Zara.

I met Damian's eyes and nodded. With a snap of my fingers, the cloud hand swept Matthias forward until he was inches from my face. I tightened the clouds around him, and he gasped.

"You. Cannot. Escape," I spat each word with venom, surprised at the hatred in my voice.

Matthias's face was hollow and ashen, too defeated to exhibit anything like shock or fury or remorse.

I ripped away my tattered sleeve and shoved it into

his mouth. "And that's in case you were going to try casting a spell."

He mumbled something and struggled in the grip of the clouds.

I assumed it was biting sarcasm, so I squeezed harder for good measure, and he groaned sharply.

"Let me make this clear. Your daughter is the only reason you're still alive."

His eyes widened in horror, and my stomach churned. I fought through my unease. "But that scenario depends on you cooperating. Hand over the genies."

He growled a muffled *"no"* through the wad of cloth.

I closed my fist, and he moaned in pain. My ribs were broken and every breath I took hurt, so I was damn keen to repay the favor.

I leaned close as he writhed. "Is it really worth taking them to your grave? They won't help you anymore, here or there."

He glared for several seconds, fury and pain burning in his eyes. Then his whole body slumped. He tried moving a hand, so I relaxed my grip.

Matthias summoned an ornate bronze box from the ether, and I quickly took it from him. He was gagged, but I wasn't taking any chances.

It was the box Damian and I had retrieved from the caverns in Cappadocia, the one I'd used to trap the djinn.

The box was ruined. The metal was twisted and

burnt, and the hinges were broken. I could still sense a hint of frankincense and tobacco, but I could tell from the signature the djinn was truly gone.

I'd destroyed one of my own kind.

That killed me inside, but Damian had given him a chance at freedom once. The djinn had kidnapped Rhiannon and four others. He'd tried to murder and entrap me.

The djinn had been a monster, but he hadn't asked to become Matthias's tool. Guilt crystalized in my gut. I was going to have to face it one day, but not today.

Today, I had to put things right.

I handed the broken box to Damian. "Where is the other one? The marid."

Matthias shot daggers at me with his eyes. A sharp squeeze set him gagging on the wadded cloth, reminding him who was in control.

He summoned the ivory bottle we'd recovered from Helwan.

Then the bastard dropped it.

The bottle spiraled down through the sky. I stopped it midair with a small eddy of wind. I was queen of the sky, after all. Still, it was a dick move.

Damian scoffed. "You're really an asshole, Matthias."

A trace of delight flickered in the iron mage's eyes.

It didn't matter.

I retrieved the bottle. It was still intact, and I could

sense that the marid was alive. And now, mine to command.

Damian pulled a couple of long, heavy zip ties from his back pocket and bound Matthias hands and feet as I looked down at the portal below.

Smoke and bursts of magic surrounded the great ring. Our battle wasn't over.

"I have to close the gateway. Take him!" I shoved Matthias into Damian's arms and raced toward the portal.

Fates, let Rhiannon be okay.

I clenched the genie bottle in my hands. Wishes could fix a lot, but they couldn't bring someone back from the dead.

The island was scarred by streaks of blood and traces of magic. My friends were huddled in a circle beneath the giant ring. Demons were everywhere.

Rage tore through me, and my strength returned. I called the storm and dropped on the demonic hordes like a cyclone. I created a pocket of calm around my friends, while the violent wind ripped the attacking demons off their feet and flung them into the sky.

With no time to lose, I shot forward to the ring. Unstable magic crackled around it, and only a few of the runes were still alight.

It was almost shut.

Then my breath caught. An extinguished rune

flashed to life, suddenly glowing with bright magic. And then another.

Demons were repairing the spells from the other side.

I had to shut the gateway now.

Releasing the hurricane, I drew upon the full strength of my magic. I thought of Magic Side, my friends, and what would happen if I couldn't shut the portal. Rage consumed me, and I could feel my magic vibrating in the air.

I summoned my khanjar and rammed it into the center of a rune. I began to speak the spell of locking that Ethan had taught me, but only two words left my mouth, booming like a thunderclap.

"Be Sealed."

Magic ripped through my body, the blade, and into the rune. Lightning danced across the surface of the ring, and with a deafening crack, all the runes went out.

Thin trails of smoke rose from the ring.

It was done.

I was finally getting the hang of this genie magic thing. Ears ringing, I whirled around.

Angels were cutting down the last of the demons who hadn't been hurled from the island.

Rhiannon was there amidst it all, grinning like a buffoon when she caught my gaze. "Holy shit, Neve! I think we lived! Did you catch that asshole?"

I ran over and wrapped my arms around her. "We got him."

As if in answer to her question, Damian alighted nearby, Matthias in tow.

I released my friend. Her hair was matted down, and she was covered head to toe with demon blood. Blue, green, every color you could think of.

"Fates," I whispered. "What happened to you? You look like hell spooged all over you."

She blanched. "Kind of what happened."

"Are you hurt?" Her clothes and tactical vest were tattered.

"Pretty badly, a couple times. It's going leave a couple of cool scars, but Nathaniel healed me during the battle," she purred.

Oh fates. She was in trouble. Or he was, I couldn't be certain.

I looked over, and Nathaniel gave me a cold nod. "We are victorious. The angels thank you."

Gods, and I thought Damian had been cold and formal once. This guy was like an incredibly beautiful ice sculpture.

Ethan strode over and placed his hands on the ring. "Neve. That was amazing. But I think you should feel this."

Damian shoved Matthias into Nathaniel's hands and joined my side as I walked back to the ring. We both laid a hand on the runes. They vibrated with foul magic.

Ethan grimaced. "Do you feel that? They're still trying to restore it from the other side. We need to destroy this gateway, now."

My stomach dropped.

So, it wasn't over, after all.

27

Damian

Ethan's words chilled me to the bone.

My skin burned from the corrupt and rancid magic that was trying to force its way back through. Ethan was right. They were trying to open the portal.

If we wanted this victory to mean anything, there was work to do.

I touched Neve gently on the shoulder. "Could you destroy it? With your power? The same way you sealed it?"

She was a living hurricane. I didn't doubt that she could rip the citadel down. I didn't doubt anything about her anymore.

Neve thought for a moment, and then slowly shook her head. "Destroying it won't be enough, Damian. They could rebuild it. We need to shut down this operation for good."

Matthias shouted something through his gag, and Nathaniel decked him across the chin. That shut him up.

Neve came close. "We should use a wish to seal it forever."

I tensed. "That will be dangerous. Do you feel confident you could control it?"

"I think I'm figuring things out, but I'm beyond drained from my battle with Matthias and sealing the portal. I need time to recover. Time, I don't think we have." She held up the genie bottle and looked at me. "But...maybe we can use the marid. How exactly do these things work?"

My gut clenched. "Neve, this is madness. I've made four wishes. None of them worked out the way I'd intended. The marid is our enemy. He would twist our words."

Determination flared in her eyes. "I need to set things right. This, I can handle. Tell me what to do."

Every fiber of my being railed against the idea, but I trusted her more than anyone in the world. "Whoever holds the bottle can take control of the genie, though he may disobey the intent of your words. If you are certain this is what you want to do, just rub the bottle and call forth the marid."

"That's it?" she asked.

I shrugged. It was a rather poor security system for something that amounted to a weapon of mass destruction.

I held my breath as Neve uncorked the bottle, rubbed it with her hand, and called out, "Great marid, I summon you to my aid."

Her voice boomed with command.

After a second, water began to drip from the mouth of the bottle onto the ice. It poured out faster and faster until it became a torrent, swirling in the air.

The marid formed before us. His eyes were piercing and infinitely blue. The ocean roared in my ears, and the scent of the sea and old wood washed over me. I could taste salt and sweet herbs. His magic was cold, not like frost, but like the abyss.

I felt the efreet's magic rise with hatred inside of me, but I reined it in.

The marid's voice rolled over us like a tidal wave, wrought with pain and fury. "I see you have defeated my old master, young djinn. So be it. You are my new master, and I owe you three wishes. Tell me, why have you summoned me from my slumber amongst the dark waves?"

Neve's eyes flared with white light, and her words roared like the wind. Her voice was low, rumbling, and everywhere at once. "I'm your master, marid, and you are at my command. Don't toy with me, or try to trick me, because I've already destroyed an efreet and a djinn, and I'll destroy you, too."

"Then what do you wish, genie-killer?"

Her body tensed so subtly that I doubted anyone else noticed. But I'd studied her every expression and knew them by heart. She was bleeding inside, but her eyes betrayed no pain.

She growled. "Tell me what you desire most."

He stared so intently at her that it felt like his eyes were peeling back her soul. At last, he spoke.

"My freedom." He turned and glared at Matthias. "And vengeance."

"And if you had to choose one?" Neve's threatening voice brought him back to attention.

The marid did not hesitate. "Freedom above all. You have no idea what it is like to be bound for centuries. To be waiting in darkness. Endless silence. Grant me my freedom. I will grant myself vengeance."

His voice roared like the ocean, a churning storm of fury and pain and madness.

My heart ached. That could have been Neve. We'd come so close to disaster. If Matthias had trapped her, he would have commanded her to kill me, to kill Rhiannon, and to destroy the city she loved.

She would have gone mad in centuries of silent guilt.

Every part of my soul wanted to grab her and take her from this place. I couldn't bear the thought of her facing down the monster she might have become.

Neve rose into the air, power crackling around her. "We once let the djinn go free, and he turned on us. You hunted us across the Earth. You tried to kill us, attacked the prison, attacked the Archives, and tried to destroy Magic Side. What will you do with your freedom?"

"Seek justice. I would rebuild that which I destroyed, and I would destroy those who brought me pain," the marid growled, rage and excitement and delight infecting his words.

Matthias struggled in Nathaniel's grasp.

Storm clouds boiled behind Neve. "What was done to you is beyond evil and can never be forgiven. But we cannot trust you as you are. Tell me, you crave vengeance, but would you trade your pain and hatred for your freedom?"

"I do not understand."

"Choose—hatred or freedom."

"Freedom."

"Then, great marid, I promise as another genie to unbind you and grant your freedom with my third wish. But for my first, I wish that you would forget your long years of suffering, forget those who have hurt you, forget your desire for vengeance, and remember only the good that you did and those who were kind to you."

The marid recoiled, rising like a wave. He looked around, stunned.

My breath caught. By wishing he would forget his suffering, Neve had placed his fate in his hands. The marid could twist the spell and cling to his rage, or choose a new life for himself. One free from the long years of suffering.

The marid closed his eyes, and a gentle rain began to fall.

His signature changed. The stench of the marine growth faded, replaced by the scent of fresh water. It no longer felt cold like the abyss, but soft, like heavy fog.

I was awed.

I could almost feel the rain wash away my pain and rage, though I knew those were my burdens to carry.

The marid looked down at Neve. "You have changed everything for me."

Truth rang in his words. The pain and madness and vindictiveness were gone.

Neve shook her head. "You have changed everything for yourself. I just made the wish."

He bowed low.

"Now, marid friend. For my second wish, I wish that you would seal this realm, so that no one may ever create a connection between it and the hells."

The rain ceased and the marid rose like a tidal wave. He crashed into the gateway, shattering it, and washed the fragments over the edge of the island.

The waters swirled, and he rose from the whirlpool. He raised his hands to the sky, and it changed from purple to blue as a powerful wave of magic crashed over us.

His voice roared like a waterfall. "It is done. No connection to the hells is possible."

"Thank you," Neve said.

Matthias started shouting through the gag and struggling.

"What?" I growled.

He mumbled something. I assumed he wasn't too keen on the marid getting free with the next wish—not after what Matthias had made him do.

To be honest, I was worried myself. Neve's first wish had stripped him of his madness, but my experience with the djinn hung heavy on my mind.

There was nothing stopping the marid from betraying us. Or at least, seeking vengeance on Matthias.

I had to trust her.

But that, for all my fears, was the easiest thing in the world.

Neve's voice boomed across the island. "Marid, I will set you free. Do you promise to seek no vengeance and to repair the damage you have done?"

He flowed to her. "I swear it. If you do this thing, my gratitude will be eternal."

She nodded. Light blazed in her eyes. "Then, marid, with my third wish, I set you free of all your bonds."

My breath left my lungs.

The marid rose on a spiraling column of water and spread his hands out. The gold bands around his wrists cracked and fell away, and the collar around his throat shattered into a thousand beads. The island shook.

His signature poured over us like the raging ocean. Never had it been so strong, even at the height of his fury.

"I am free!" His body crashed into the ground like a wave, and then he reformed like a god emerging from the primordial waters. He turned to Neve. "Thank you for this, my friend. I will always be grateful."

The island shook again, and hairline cracks formed at my feet.

Matthias wrenched free of Nathaniel's grasp and rammed his shoulder into my chest. I grabbed him and spun him around. "Do you want me to toss you over the edge? I'll—"

He started shouting through the gag. Panic and pleading flashed in his eyes.

I yanked Neve's shirt sleeve out of his mouth. "You've got ten seconds. What is it?"

Matthias gritted his teeth. "You idiots! The connection with the hells was the only thing keeping the realm from descending into utter chaos. We need to get out of here, now! Think *Titanic*."

The panic in his voice raised the hairs on my neck. I'd known him for centuries. This was serious. I spun and shouted, "Time to go. This place is about to fall apart!"

As if to punctuate my words, the ice island suddenly

groaned and cracked beneath our feet. A fragment broke off and began drifting into the sky.

Gods. Damned. Wishes.

The ice quaked.

The Searing Citadel shuddered on the island of ice.

The wolves.

I hurled Matthias into the arms of one of the angels. "Get him, Ethan, and Rhiannon back to Magic Side."

"Where are you going?" he asked.

Ignoring him, I grabbed Neve by the arm. "Say goodbye to your new friend. Jaxson and his team are still in the tower. They've got transport charms, but we need to make sure they get out!"

Nathaniel scooped up Rhiannon in his arms, while another angel grabbed Ethan. A flurry of silver smoke filled the air, and Neve, the marid, and I were the only ones left on the island.

"Get out of here!" Neve yelled to the marid.

He scooped up a fragment of the bottle and tossed it into her hands. "If you ever need me, concentrate on that and ask. I will come if I can."

With that, he formed into a wave and crashed down into mist.

Neve and I leapt into the air and soared toward the citadel. I reached out with my dragon sense. Jaxson was still here.

We landed on a balcony. Neve waved her hand, and

the iron door blasted off its hinges. We raced down the halls.

The place was deserted. I followed my dragon sense back to the teleportation chamber. The wolves were assembled around the ring.

"What the hell took you guys so long?" Jaxson growled, "This place is falling apart!"

"Did you get the prisoners?" Neve asked, chest heaving.

He pointed at a huddled group of people. "And some extras. Order folks that Matthias kidnapped as well. We scoured the place. Demons are gone. We were just about to leave."

I clapped him on the shoulder. "I owe you more than you could imagine. Time to go."

He nodded. The wolves each grabbed one of the ex-prisoners, and transport charms exploded around us in silver plumes of magic.

I scanned the room. We were the last ones.

It was over.

I grabbed Neve's arms. She looked up and raised her eyebrows. "Nothing like escaping a collapsing tower to put a cherry on the day. Why don't we ever go anywhere relaxing?"

I smiled and brushed her hair from her face. "Let's go home. I've got some things in mind."

She closed her eyes, and the cosmos roared around us.

28

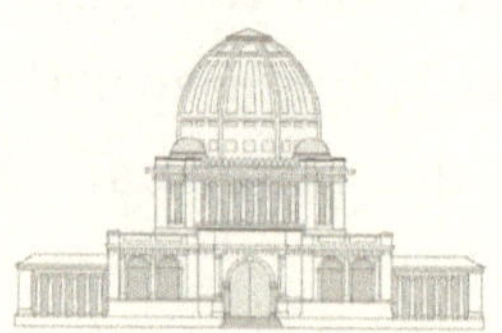

Neve

The ether spat us out in the square fronting the Hall of Inquiry. Damian had managed to heal my wounds during our planes-walk, and the pain from earlier was gone.

The angels gracefully alighted around us as shifters appeared in puffs of silver smoke.

Jaxson immediately crouched down by one of the wounded shifters, and Ethan rushed to the prisoners, checking them for wounds. Everyone looked bruised and battered.

A cocktail of adrenaline and shock were still coursing through my body, and I knew as soon as I relaxed, every part of me was going to feel raw.

Rhia was still in Nathaniel's arms, and she gazed up at him longingly. "After planes-walking with you guys for three weeks, I can conclusively say that I'd much rather travel with Nathaniel."

My jaw hung open. Never, ever, in a thousand years would I have imagined Rhia letting someone carry her like that.

Nathaniel cast her a seductive look and lowered her to her feet. "You fought bravely today."

I laughed as she swayed—probably from shock but also because angels had that kind of effect.

"Where will you take him?" I asked Nathaniel, gesturing to Matthias who was slouched between two angels, his hands now bound behind his back with magicuffs.

I still couldn't believe we'd finally brought the bastard down. Half my heart expected him to vanish in a puff of smoke at any second, to trick us one last time.

"He will stand trial before the Assembly, and after he atones for his crimes, he will be placed in the Pillars of Penitence," Nathaniel said, dipping his head to the two angels holding Matthias.

They lifted him to his feet, and Matthias's face tightened in panic. "Will you tell Zara?"

I met his gaze. "I'll tell her everything. She deserves to know what a monster you are."

His expression hardened, and he nodded. Despite all he'd done, I knew he loved Zara. I'd heard it in his voice when he'd warned her to stay away from Damian the last time we'd met in his house.

It felt like months ago.

I couldn't help but feel a little pity for him. "She loves you, despite everything."

Matthias hung his head.

The hum of bells rose around us, and suddenly, Matthias and the angels at his side disappeared in a flash of light.

Just like that, it was over.

Truly over.

I was free.

Nathaniel handed Damian a small black box that was oddly familiar. "Farewell brother. Perhaps you will visit us again."

Damian took the box, and I recognized it as the one he'd pocketed right before we planes-walked to Armenia. He opened it a crack, and gold flashed in the light.

He shook his head and gripped arms with the angel, pulling him close. "Even if my life depended on it, I wouldn't return to the Order of Angels. But you know where to find me. Visit anytime."

Nathaniel chuckled and glanced at Rhiannon, who had sidled up next to me. "Perhaps I will."

"Sweet heavens, yes," Rhia whispered, her cheeks flushed.

I choked back a laugh and cleared my throat as Nathaniel bowed his head to me. "Until we meet again, Nevaeh."

He'd finally addressed me by my name and not child.

Perhaps he wasn't so bad. He'd helped us close the gateway after all, and I'd seen how he'd protected Rhiannon when the battle had gotten rough—though he may have had his own motivations for doing so.

I dipped my head. "Thanks, Nathaniel. Hope to see you around."

The hum of bells rose in the air, and Nathaniel vanished in a brilliant flash of light.

"That man is intense, but holy mother of angels," Rhia said with a smirk on her face.

"I thought shifters were your thing."

"They are so last week. But..." She tracked Jaxson as he approached Damian. "*Who* is that beast?"

"Jaxson? He's the son of the dockside alpha." If the angels were beautiful, Jaxson was another kind of gorgeous. Built like a firetruck with broad shoulders and a muscular build, his dark, wavy hair that matched his eyes and the six o'clock shadow on his jaw were all kinds of right. In other words, *one hundred percent man hunk*. Nathaniel had nothing on him, and Rhia was speechless.

Damian shook Jaxson's hand. "Thanks. I owe you and the pack. Let me know what you need."

"I'd say we're square, but there might be some future business dealings we could use your insights on. We'll be in touch." Jaxson nodded at me and Rhia, and he and his shifters crossed to several trucks that had pulled up beside the park.

"I was mistaken. Shifters are so in," Rhia whispered, watching Jaxson climb into the truck and drive off.

I shook my head and smiled at Damian, who was *my* kind of gorgeous and one hundred percent mine.

"Well, we did it, and we didn't die," Rhia said. "I'd say that calls for a celebration. Early happy hour at the Hideout? First round's on me."

Thirty minutes later, we were on our second round of shots at the Hideout.

"Cheers!" Ethan, Rhia, Gretchen, and Damian and I clinked our shot glasses together.

I pulled mine back, clenching my teeth as the tequila burned my throat. Being a full djinn meant that the alcohol didn't affect me as much, which was a good thing because I was also nursing my second G&T.

Slamming my shot glass on the bar top, I wheeled around on my tall barstool. It was happy hour from four to six, and folks were beginning to pack in. Rhia was cracking a joke at Ethan, and Gretchen was chatting up the bartender, Diana. Warmth flooded my chest. I was home and everything was right in the world.

On our way over, I'd told Gretchen that I'd be taking a few months off from work. I needed to make up for the time that I'd missed with my parents and figure out the whole being-a-crazy-powerful-genie thing.

Rather than asking for a resignation letter, she'd squeezed my shoulder and promoted me to detective. *On a contractual basis.* It was more than I could have hoped for, and I'd nearly cried in front of the L.T.

I cringed at the thought.

Of course, I hadn't told Gretchen the primary reason I needed some time off. My eyes locked onto Damian. He broke off his conversation with a patron, and I swayed back and forth on the barstool as he slowly closed the distance between us.

Clutching the front of his shirt, I gently pulled him close so he was positioned right between my legs. "What was inside the box that Nathaniel gave you?"

He smiled and drew the box from his pocket, handing it to me. It was black and velvety, and inside was a golden necklace with a round pendant. I raised my eyebrow at him. "What is it?"

"The insignia of the angels. I kept it after my fall."

"But why did you give it to Nathaniel?"

Damian's eyes glinted. "My atonement was forfeiting my angel. I didn't need the reminder of what I'd lost."

"I don't understand."

"I gave up my angelic magic."

My stomach churned as the implications set in. Rage trickled through my veins.

"You fool!" I hissed. "Are you serious? You gave up your magic, like your ability to heal?"

He nodded. "It was the only option."

I grabbed his lapel and yanked him close. "And. You. Didn't. Tell. Me."

Guilt flickered in his eyes. "Never again."

I wanted to hold onto my anger, but it slipped through my fingers. Damian had given up a part of himself to strike a deal with the angels. To save us. The weight of that pressed down on me, and guilt and sadness pooled in my chest.

"You should have told me, Damian," I whispered.

He took my hands in his and pressed a kiss on them. "You had enough on your shoulders as it was."

"But you had flaming wings. You flew. How?"

He shook his head. "It turns out, what the djinn told me was true. You can't change what you are. You can only change what you choose to do with the powers you're given."

My heart skipped about five beats. "You still have your angelic magic then?"

A smile graced his lips, and my heartbeat thundered against my chest. "That's right,

but it's nothing compared to what you did today. You were extraordinary."

.   .   .

"It wasn't me. It was all of us." I looked around the bar, filled with my friends. A sense of relief and joy flooded through me.

Damian lifted my chin. "It was you. Magic like I never imagined. And you did the right thing with the marid."

I frowned. "You would have done the same for him. It's what you did with the djinn."

Damian shook his head. "No. It's not. I freed the djinn without considering the consequences or what he might have gone through—and that nearly cost you your best friend. You took away the marid's suffering and gave him a new life. You have a special heart."

I bit my lip. "I just couldn't shake the thought of what would have happened to me if Matthias had caught me. I think I would have gone mad."

Damian brushed my hair back and smiled. "But you got away. How did you break Matthias's spell, anyway? One moment, he was draining your power, and the next he was at your mercy."

I shrugged. "I'm not sure. I figured my only chance was to bind myself, to cast the spell before him. But my words came out as something more than just a spell. It felt like I was waking up from a dream, and I realized something that I should have learned a long time ago. That I was my own master—of my emotions, of my wishes, and of my fate. Maybe that's something every djinn has to learn. Something Queen Mavia couldn't just put into words."

Pride crossed his face, and he slid his hands over my knees. "So, Miss Cross, does this mean you are a queen now? Do you plan to retire to a floating frost palace and tend to a garden of ice sculptures?"

I laughed. "Oh, hell no."

But what to do next was a good question. Life ahead of me was an open book.

I could have it all.

I licked my lips. "Well, I wouldn't mind a palace really... but not one of ice, and definitely no mazes. And rather than an ice garden, I want to create something that gives back."

He grinned, and I traced the curve of his lips. "And what might that be?"

A temple for what I cherished most—*knowledge.*

"A library in the sky. We know so little about the planes—so maybe I'll build an archive dedicated to unexplored worlds. A place open and accessible to *all* Magica who wish to visit it. And I insist, it will be organized by imps."

Damian tilted his head back and laughed, a deep rumble erupting from his chest. Gods he was gorgeous. "I should have known. In that case, I'll be your first patron."

He drew the Atlas of the Planes from the ether and handed it to me. "My gift to you, Nevaeh. May it guide you to the furthest reaches of the realms in search of your books."

My heart swelled and something lodged in my throat. "This is perfect. Thank you. But it will guide *us*. I expect you by my side."

He gently cupped my face with his hand, tracing his thumb over my cheekbone. "Of course, Nevaeh. I will always be at your side, through thick or thin. You are my treasure, and I'm not letting you out of my sight."

Happiness and pride filled me. Damian had changed so much since we'd met. He'd conquered his darkness and accepted what couldn't be changed, and I guess in a way, so had I. We'd slain our demons together.

I swallowed the tightness in my throat, not wanting to spoil this moment with tears, because, yeah, being a genie made me emotional.

"Then it's settled," he said. "We'll build a library and fill it with all the books we can find."

I thought of the Library of Alexandria and silently cringed. "Legally and ethically, you mean."

"Of course. Who do you think I am, a book thief?"

Probably.

I choked out a laugh. My heart was overflowing.

"But first, Mr. Malek, before we do any of that"—I slid my hand over his chest and, grabbing the collar of his shirt, I slowly tugged him down, so his face was inches from mine—"I want a repeat of last night."

His eyes flashed with desire. He leaned forward and dragged his mouth over my neck. I shivered under his touch and dipped my head back, delighting in the way his spicy pine scent skated over my skin, stroking over my nerves like the first time we'd met.

"How about right now?" His whiskey voice sent liquid heat straight to my center.

I nodded and wrapped my arms around him. The ether sucked us in and Rhia and the others faded away as we shot through the cosmos like a burning comet.

The spinning stopped, and I opened my eyes. The fireplace crackled and candles blazed around the room of the cabin.

Damian lowered me onto the bed, planting his arms on either side of me. "What exactly did you want repeated from last night?"

"I don't recall. Why don't you remind me?" I wrapped my arms around his neck and pulled his mouth to mine.

"Your wish is my command."

Thanks for joining us on this adventure!

Our next COMPLETED series is out now! Prepare for shifters and more romance! Sink your teeth into Wolf Marked, here: mybook.to/Wolf-Marked

Or, begin our newest series, Ruthless Gods: mybook.to/Wolf-God

Want to stay in touch? Join our newsletter (you can unsubscribe at any time and we never spam!):

https://www.veronicadouglas.com/newsletter

AUTHOR'S NOTE
VERONICA DOUGLAS

Thank you for reading *Broken Skies*—we hope you enjoyed it as much as we did! While this is the last book of Neve and Damian's story, they'll be sticking around. In fact, this is only the first series of many involving Magic Side and its characters.

You've already met the hero of our next book, Jaxson Laurent—werewolf and son of the Dockside Alpha. He'll be making an appearance in the finale of Linsey Hall's *Wolf Queen* and features in our completed series Magic Side: Wolf Bound. Start the first book, *Wolf Marked*, here: mybook.to/Wolf-Marked

This leaves the important question: who's the heroine? She's the star of the show after all! Well, you haven't met her yet. At the moment, she's just a tough girl working in small-town Wisconsin. She has no idea how special she is, or that magic and werewolves are even real.

She might be in for a bit of a shock.

We're super excited about the Wolf Bound series, but for now, we'd like to say a few words about the history and archaeology that inspired this book. In *Wicked Wish*, when Neve and Damian visit Cappadocia, she learns he can speak Turkish. That was a little hint that he had some history in that part of the world, and hence their travels to Armenia. Neve and Damian's visit to meet Nathaniel and the Order of Angels is inspired by Tatev Monastery. It's located on a basalt plateau in southeastern Armenia and was constructed in the 9th century AD overlooking the Vorotan River gorge. One legend about the monastery is that during the church's construction, an apprentice climbed to the roof to place a cross. He fell off and plunged into the gorge and cried out to God to give him wings. In Armenian, this is "Ta Tev."

Broken Skies is set in the wider Dragon's Gift universe created by Linsey Hall. The best part of writing in this big world is that we're able to bring in characters from other series, so you can expect a lot of crossovers between the folks from Guild City, Magic's Bend, and Magic Side in the future.

Did you miss the alternate scenes from *Wicked Wish* and *Dark Storm*? Check out Damian's take on the kiss scene in the djinn's maze here: https://dl.bookfunnel.

com/ei29gyov4m. You can also read a prologue story about Damian releasing the djinn here: https://dl.book funnel.com/97k79s714b

That's all for now, but you can keep turning the pages to find out more about our next series, Magic Side: Wolf Bound.

Thank you again for reading and be sure to sign up for our newsletter for sneak peaks, extra scenes, and super exclusive content! https://www.veronicadouglas. com/newsletter

WOLF MARKED

MAGIC SIDE: WOLF BOUND BOOK 1

VERONICA DOUGLAS

WOLF BOUND: WOLF MARKED

mybook.to/Wolf-Marked

I was just an ordinary girl waiting tables in a small-town bar. I had no idea magic was real. That was, until I backed my car over a werewolf a couple times.

In my defense, the wolf was trying to murder me, and I was all out of mace.

Now I've got a cult of rogue wolves on my heels, and the only one who can protect me is Jaxson Laurent—the alpha of the Chicago pack.

He suspects I'm special and can't take his eyes off me, but the problem is—he's the sworn enemy of my family. Every time we get close it feels like something is going to rip out of my soul, but the heat between us is irresistible.

Like it or not, the fates are pushing us together.

With danger around every corner and wolves howling in the night, I need to master my magic and stand my ground, or I'll be dead before the next moon rises.

ACKNOWLEDGMENTS
VERONICA DOUGLAS

Thank you to everyone who has been so supportive, especially Lindsey and Ben—we love you guys!

Thank you to Jena O'Connor and Lexi George for your patience and amazing editing. We'd be nowhere with you.

Thank you to the amazing readers on our advanced review team! Extra special thanks to Rachel, Susie, Penny, Aisha, and Michele—your eyes are so sharp!

And finally, a huge shoutout to Jes Ireland and Orina Kafe for the gorgeous cover art.

ACKNOWLEDGMENTS

LINSEY HALL

Thank you so much to Veronica and Doug, it's still so much fun to write with you guys!

And as usual, thank you to Ben. There would be no books without you.

Thank you to Jena O'Connor and Lexi George for your amazing editing. And to Jes Ireland and Orina Kafe for the beautiful cover.

ABOUT VERONICA DOUGLAS

Veronica Douglas is a duo of professional archaeologists that love writing and digging together. After spending an inordinate amount of time doing painstaking research for academia, they suddenly discovered a passion for letting their imaginations go wild! A cocktail of magic, romance, and ancient mystery (shaken, not stirred), their books are inspired, in part, by their life in Chicago and their archaeological adventures from around the globe.

ABOUT LINSEY HALL

Before becoming a writer, Linsey Hall was a nautical archaeologist who studied shipwrecks from Hawaii and the Yukon to the UK and the Mediterranean. She credits fantasy and historical romances with her love of history and her career as an archaeologist. After a decade of tromping around the globe in search of old bits of stuff that people left lying about, she settled down and started penning her own romance novels. Her series draw upon her love of history and the paranormal elements that she can't help but include.

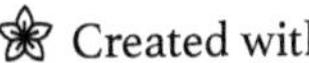 Created with Vellum

www.ingramcontent.com/pod-product-compliance
Lightning Source LLC
Chambersburg PA
CBHW051250210726
48287CB00002B/432